THE Jewel THIEF

PAULA WELCH

Typesetting and e-book design: Amit Dey (amitdey2528@gmail.com)
Cover design: Donika Mishineva (www.artofdonika.com)

ISBN number: 978-0-6459910-4-8 (paperback)

NATIONAL LIBRARY OF AUSTRALIA

A catalogue record for this book is available from the National Library of Australia

DEDICATION

I dedicate this book to my amazing sister, Alyson.
No longer in my life, but always in my heart.

SPECIAL THANKS TO

Laurel Cohn and her team,
Aurora House
&
Grace Castagnella for picking
up on my repetitive mistakes.

OTHER BOOKS
BY PAULA WELCH

<u>Children's fiction</u>

The Interlopers

<u>Adult fiction</u>

A River of Fortune

Cloud Piercer

A Goode Inheritance

CONTENTS

PROLOGUE

May 1939

He ran faster than his heart would allow. His rucksack weighed him down, and he was sweating profusely. He darted through the woods using the trees for cover. The night air had the stench of death in it. But it wouldn't be his. He had to get to the coast. From there, he would find a ship and get off this accursed island.

His mate was dead. Shot like a dog and left to bleed out. His fence was in London. On his arrival in Plymouth, he would make contact. He'd see him right.

He scurried through the night, like a fox on the run, until he found a road. After a long walk, he managed to hitch a ride in the back of a farmer's truck that carried him to Plymouth.

The following night he waited in a stench-ridden old pub until closing for his contact to arrive. He never showed. He was getting anxious, unsure of his next move. Something was wrong. His fence was never late.

When he left the pub, he headed down a narrow, dark, cobblestone lane. He kept to the shadows, away from prying eyes. But they found him. He wasn't unaccustomed to street brawls and eventually got the upper hand. Breathless, he scurried out of the alley and kept to the shadows until his ship departed the following night. He had much to do.

At last, he walked up the gangplank and boarded the *Jervis Bay*. Once safely on board, he turned around and looked out over Plymouth.

'Good fucking riddance,' he mumbled under his breath. Then he turned his back on England for the last time.

In a narrow, dark, cobblestone lane, the bodies of two men that had been dumped in a sewer drain, would not be found for more than a year.

Chapter One

Jubilee Jones felt like a lost soul floating through a sea of insecurity even before the pandemic wreaked havoc and robbed her of a thriving career. After losing her job as head chef at The Mariner in Sydney, Jubilee was forced to return to her family home in Bowral, a small town nestled in the southern highlands of New South Wales.

Her childhood home wasn't a stately manor, but it was filled with the usual childhood memories. Some good, some bad. You could describe it as a renovator's delight. A real fixer-upper old fibro house.

For Jubilee, ever since childhood, life had been an expression of art. She used to paint the world in many colours until she found a greater love in cooking. Now, as an adult, she loved to create delicious culinary feasts. Unlike the great artworks pinned to the walls of museums for all to admire each passing year, Jubilee's artwork only lasted as long as it took the customer to consume it.

Reluctantly, over a year ago, Jubilee gave up her apartment in Sydney, as her dwindling savings had been devoured by the overpriced apartment she rented. She feared the pandemic would outlive what remained of her savings, and finally gave up on returning to The Mariner when she received word that it would never re-open.

Now, sitting on a garden chair with her feet hunched up in front of her, Jubilee felt fractured and alone. She wore a beanie to ward off the chilly June morning air and cover her thick, wavy, shoulder-length dark brown hair. A scarf was wrapped around her neck for extra warmth. With her hands clasped around a hot cup of tea, she watched the steam blow away with the wind, and realised it was a metaphor for her life. Out of habit, she twirled a ring around her finger absentmindedly. It had been a gift from her grandmother for her 21st birthday.

In truth, Jubilee's lack of *joie de vivre* had nothing to do with her job prospects. Long before COVID, Jubilee had felt distant and detached from life. If she had to describe her maudlin state, she would liken it to always walking two steps behind everyone else and not having the will to keep up.

At times, she wanted to cry. She had loved her job at The Mariner, had great friends, short-lived but romantic love affairs, and a great apartment in Sydney, but in all that success, something was awry. She felt as if she didn't belong there. In truth, she didn't know where she belonged at times.

Jubilee's spirit was restless. If it was trying to tell her something, she hadn't figured it out yet. Now, back home in Bowral, she was too comfortable and stagnant. She needed her cage rattled.

On her return to Bowral, Jubilee had found a part-time job working in a local bakery. A year on, with COVID mostly behind her, Jubilee had to decide if she should return to Sydney.

She was a gifted chef, but there were far more experienced chefs now in Sydney than restaurants. In truth, she should have started searching months ago, but her heart wasn't in it. There were restaurants in Bowral and around the Southern Highlands, however, she would just be going through the same motions, only in a different town.

Jubilee had been grateful for her mother's company since arriving home. However, when the restrictions were over, and travel resumed, Mauve and her fiancé Marcus, headed up to his holiday home, in the tropical paradise of Mackay.

On their last video call, Mauve announced they had decided to live up there permanently.

Jubilee was truly happy for her mum, but she wished she was with her in Bowral. Mauve always knew how to guide Jubilee through her melancholic states and talking on video wasn't quite as good as the real thing.

During their last video chat, Mauve announced that she was giving Jubilee their home in Bowral. Her mother had said she'd inherit it one day anyway, so she might as well have it now.

'Live there, or sell it, and use the money to start your own restaurant,' Mauve said. 'It's time you look to the future.'

Mauve suggested she put her morose energy into renovating the house and garden. If she decided to return to Sydney, the property would sell for a better price if the gardens looked more like gardens rather than weed-infested bushland.

Jubilee was grateful to her mum for giving her their family home. It gave her options. But Jubilee was still unsure what the right option was. Finally, she agreed with her mum and drew up a plan to restore the gardens. After her shift at the bakery, Jubilee spent her spare time weeding, re-potting and planting for the upcoming spring. Regrettably, not knowing a weed from wildflower, she decided to stick to vegetables, and created a vegetable garden.

Her mother was right of course; the exhilarating cold fresh air was just what Jubilee and the garden needed.

It's remarkable though, how life can change so dramatically when you least expect it.

On one particular frosty June morning, Jubilee emptied the garden shed of all its rubbish and tossed it into a skip she had hired. The old doghouse was barely standing. With little effort, she knocked it down and threw all the old wooden slats into the skip. A plaque that read *Finn* was still attached to the front of the doghouse. It wasn't the name of Jubilee's dog as a child, so she assumed Finn belonged to her mother or grandparents. Jubilee wondered if Finn was named after Huckleberry Finn – it had been her grandfather's favourite book.

After mowing the lawn, Jubilee decided to tackle a row of dead rose bushes. By the afternoon, she had dug up what she was sure were dead bushes and thrown them in the skip. She thought her vegetable patch would fit in nicely along the fence where they had once resided. Rummaging through the shed until she found some wooden poles and string to map out two rectangles for her vegetable garden, Jubilee picked up the shovel and turned the soil over.

Despite the chilly air, Jubilee started to sweat and realised she wasn't as fit as she thought she was. Eventually, she dug her shovel deep into the soil and hit something hard. It wasn't rock, the sound was metallic. For good measure, Jubilee lunged the shovel down again. Something clanked.

Jubilee tossed the shovel aside and got down on her hands and knees. With her hands, she dug the soil away. Finally, an old canvas bag revealed itself. Digging around its sides, she pulled it free. She opened the bag to reveal a large biscuit tin.

The old-fashioned tin read *Arnott's Biscuits*.

It felt heavy for a biscuit tin. Jubilee assumed it was full of soil. When she shook the tin, it rattled. She grimaced and wondered if she had just dug up an old family pet.

'I hope you're not Finn,' she said to the tin.

When she was a child, Jubilee had a dog. When he died, her mother had it cremated. His ashes were scattered in the garden where he used to like sleeping. No, she thought, the tin was too small to fit a pet dog inside. Maybe a cat, though!

Jubilee gave the tin another shake but it didn't sound like bones, but then again, she didn't know what rattling bones sounded like either. She wondered if it was a time capsule. Someone must have put it there and forgotten about it. *How cool*, she thought. Maybe her mother or her Aunt Joan had buried it when they were children.

Jubilee tried to open the tin, but years of corrosion wouldn't let it budge. She went into the house to find something to pry it open.

Using a good knife, after breaking an old one, Jubilee finally managed to prise the lid open. Resting inside the tin was a purple velvet cloth. Delicately, she unfolded the cloth, afraid she might uncover tiny skeletal remains.

Jubilee jumped back.

After taking a moment to recover, she slowly took a step toward the tin and had another peep inside, just in case her mind was playing tricks on her. Her mouth remained open as she gazed down at the tin. Surreal, dreamlike even, she looked down in wonder.

Jewels!

Lots of ornate, expensive-looking jewellery.

Necklaces, earrings, bracelets, rings and even a tiara. Jewels of every colour: reds, greens and blues sparkled up at her from within the tin. She also saw pearls and diamonds.

Carefully, Jubilee picked up each piece of jewellery and examined it. Were they real? Why would anyone bury fake jewellery?

'Holy fuck!' she exclaimed.

Jubilee took a clean tea towel from a kitchen drawer and dampened it. She bathed and delicately cleaned each piece as she would a newborn baby's head.

Still in shock, she spread each item out on the dining room table. There were eighteen items in total.

Four necklaces.

One tiara.

Two bracelets.

Four sets of earrings.

Five rings.

A pendant and a brooch.

One ring had the largest diamond she had ever seen. If it was real, that is. But what caught her eye was a magnificent ruby. It sparkled up at her, sitting prominently in the heart of a necklace. She'd never seen one that size before. That's when she noticed the matching set of earrings, bracelet and ring that accompanied it. She placed them side-by-side as they deserved to be together.

Jubilee wasn't sure what to do. Should she call the police? How did they get there? Who put them there? Did the rule, 'finders keepers' apply? Jubilee couldn't imagine for a moment that her mother knew anything about the old biscuit tin. She would have dug it up years ago to pay for the leaking roof. If they didn't belong to her family, then who?

With all the excitement, Jubilee hadn't noticed a paper bag sitting in the bottom of the biscuit tin. She opened it. Inside was an old passport, in the name of: *Jack Hawthorn, Cornwall, England.*

Who was this man? She didn't recognise the name, nor knew anything about Cornwall. As she flicked through the passport, an old picture fell out. It was a black and white photo of a family she didn't recognise. When she turned the picture over, at the top left-hand corner, there was a hand-written note: *Hawthorn Manor – March, 1939.*

There was another notation, in the bottom right-hand corner, written in a different ink and hand: *1948 CBBBS*

Jubilee was struggling to know what to do. She doubted they belonged to her grandparents. The only valuable asset they ever owned was the land her house was sitting on. Jubilee resolved to notify the police.

Judiciously, Jubilee put everything back in the Arnott's biscuit tin, then hid it in her wardrobe at the far back and covered it with a pile of jumpers. Then she called her mum, who was just as shocked by the discovery as Jubilee. Mauve had said that if her parents had put it there, they would have told her. Jubilee was becoming more curious by the minute. Mauve told her daughter to tread carefully in whatever she decided to do. They both knew handing the jewellery over to the police was the right call, as they would discover who the rightful owners were faster than she could. However, Jubilee had questions she doubted the police would delve too deeply into: why were they buried in my garden? How long ago? And, by whom?

That night, Jubilee sat by the fireplace in her small living room, watching the wood crackle in the grate. She opened her laptop and looked up Arnott's Biscuits online to see when they began manufacturing that particular tin. Her searches revealed it was first sold in 1934.

Then Jubilee checked the land title registry, which only told her the name of the current owner of her property. In that moment, she decided to head to the local council's office in the morning to find out who owned the land before her grandparents. Hopefully, she could trace the past occupants and figure out who buried the tin.

At that moment her mobile chimed, telling her she had a message.

From Meg:

Hi, Jubes. How does your garden grow? Any silver bells and cockle shells? 🌱

Jubilee smiled, she didn't know how she would have coped this last year without her cousin's humour and friendship.

From Jubilee:

Fat chance, but I dug up more than I expected. Talk Soon. 🐱

Unable to sleep, Jubilee lay awake all night with a hundred different questions. Oddly, she felt as if a thousand eyes were boring down upon her. She got up twice to check that the tin was still in the cupboard, snuggled under a mound of jumpers, where she hid it.

Before she fell asleep, Jubilee had resolved one dilemma. She would not go to the police just yet. She needed to uncover the truth about her biscuit tin for herself. There was a story behind these hidden jewels, she didn't want to hear clinical answers that the police would provide. This was her story to unravel.

However, if she couldn't find any answers to this mystery, she would go to the police and report her discovery.

Jubilee had fallen asleep with a fire in her belly, something she hadn't felt for a very long time.

Chapter Two

Wingecarribee Shire Council

June 9 – Friday

Jubilee made herself scrambled eggs on toast and a coffee before heading to the council's office. She left the house with a spring in her step. She could feel something dormant stirring within her, but she wasn't frightened or melancholic. She decided to see where the river took her. To stream's end, or out to sea and the unknown.

Jubilee arrived at her local council as they opened. She approached the customer service representative, who still wore a facemask even though it wasn't compulsory any longer.

'How can I help you today?' she asked, from behind her mask.

Hoping rather than believing, Jubilee asked for a list of the previous owners of her property.

'I would love to, but we can't give out that information due to the Privacy Act,' she replied.

'Is there a way around the Privacy Act?'

'I'll pretend I didn't hear that,' she said. Jubilee couldn't tell if she was smiling behind the mask or not. 'However, if your house had any renovations done, or if the owners applied for a shed, that sort of thing, then you can submit a previous development application form to see who applied for it and when. Or failing that, you could try a third party such as an architectural firm or builder. Plus, there is also the Berrima Historical Society. They hold property information. Is your home an historical building?'

'No,' Jubilee said with a smirk. No one had ever classified her little fibro home as historical or heritage listed for that matter. 'Where do I go for a previous development application?'

'You will need to go to our Corporate Information Department, if you want to trace back prior to June 2010.'

Jubilee thanked her before being directed to the right department. She filled in the form and was told to expect a reply within seven days.

Jubilee decided to head home and finish off the back garden while she waited for a reply. For the remainder of the day, Jubilee dug up every flowerbed in the back garden enthusiastically, eager to see if anything else was buried there. Alas, she dug in vain, uncovering only a couple of old forgotten dog bones, three odd socks, two shoes of different sizes, and a squeaky toy in the shape of a bone with a broken chain on it.

There would have been dozens of builders and architects in the Southern Highlands district over the decades. She doubted most would still be operating, but thought it was worth a try. After a long hot bath, and a warming dinner, she hopped back on her laptop and started searching.

That evening, sitting alone by the fireplace once again, disappointed by her lack of progress, Jubilee telephoned a friend to tell them what she had discovered, but disconnected before the call went through. For now, she realised it was prudent to keep what she'd found under her hat. Jubilee remembered her mother's advice to tread carefully. Jubilee hadn't spoken to many friends back in Sydney since returning home, which was entirely her own fault. Her mood had sobered since her return to Bowral. Feeling like a failure, with no satisfying job prospects ahead, she felt despondent. She was grateful for her mother's understanding and patience. The only continual contacts she had were her mother, work colleagues at the bakery, her aunt, uncle, and cousins, Meg, Jodie and Emily in Mittagong. Finally, when permitted, the occasional visit to her grandmother who lived at the nursing home, which had now relaxed its restrictions.

The week trickled on, but each night before bed, Jubilee retrieved the biscuit tin from her wardrobe. Her excuse was to remind herself it wasn't all a dream. She smiled down at the magnificent jewels. In turn, they always sparkled back at her. Winking at her in the lamplight as if they knew something she didn't.

They were finally free from their cavernous dark cage.

Chapter Three

Jubilee's House, Bowral

June 15 – Thursday

Jubilee had finished her shift at the bakery. She sat on her porch listening to the thunder, as the rain poured down. An email had finally arrived from the Wingecarribee Shire Council. It stated an extension had been built onto the house in 1949. It listed the architect and builder. The name of the homeowner was Jack Jones, Jubilee's great-grandfather. Jubilee wasn't sure when the house was built but thought it must have been built in the late 1930s to early 1940s, so she needed to be sure if her great-grandfather had purchased the house from someone else.

Jubilee spent an hour searching the internet for the builder but hit another roadblock. She had looked up old census records and contacted the local historical society. She even called a few local realtors in the hope one of them had sold their property back in the day but only hit more roadblocks.

In the end, Jubilee called her mother to give an update on what she had uncovered. With resignation in her voice, she told her mum she would probably need to involve the police. Mauve didn't know much about her grandfather but told Jubilee to speak to her aunt Joan, as she was the family historian. If she was unable to help, then she could go to the police.

'Of course!' Jubilee exclaimed. She picked up her keys and ran out of the house. She could have kicked herself. Why hadn't she considered Aunt Joan? She would know. Jubilee arrived in Mittagong a little after 4:00 pm. Uncle Phil told Jubilee she could find Joan in the back garden doing some weeding. She thanked him and walked through the house towards the back garden finding her aunt on her knees by her beloved rose bushes.

'Hi, Aunt Joan.'

Joan looked up from her weeding. 'Jubilee, what a pleasant surprise. What brings you here?'

'I need to pick your brain about Mum's house.'

'Sure, what do you want to know?' Joan stood up with a groan and straightened her back as they walked to the garden table and sat down.

Jubilee had always adored her aunt's garden. It was a botanical feast of Australian native plants and bushes. Rose bushes wrapped around a large fountain, which had an array of water lettuce, poppies, and yellow irises in it. The fountain and roses were neatly separated from the rest of the garden by a manicured hedgerow that stood no more than three feet tall. A tranquil pond was at the bottom end of the giant garden, which was inhabited by an ever-growing family of ducks. Jubilee understood why her aunt loved to spend so much time in her garden. It was always a feast of aromas and colours, especially when spring arrived. Jubilee cringed at the thought of her own rose bushes, now dumped in the skip.

Joan poured Jubilee and herself a drink.

'I've been trying to trace the previous owners of Mum's house and she told me to ask you. I found out my great-grandfather, Jack Jones, lived there in 1949 as he had some renovations done. But I thought the house was built in the 1930s. I need to know who owned it before him.'

'That's easy. No one.'

'What?'

'Your great-grandfather, my grandfather, purchased the land in 1940 and built the house in 1942 after marrying your great-grandmother, Mary Brody. I thought you knew that.'

'No. I knew Granddad and Nana left Mum the house and you a cash settlement to the same value. But I didn't know Grandad's dad Jack Jones built it.'

'Well, yes. As Mauve was a single mum and had moved back home when your dad left, it was the obvious thing to do. She got the house and I got the cash.'

Jubilee was reminiscent for a moment at the mention of her father. She couldn't remember the last time she saw or spoke to him. Too long ago. She put him aside for the moment, but not as easily as he brushed her aside when he left.

'Can you tell me anything about Jack Jones? Do you have a picture of him, any documentation from his time in England?'

'Why the interest all of a sudden?'

'I just need to know about him. Who he was? Where did he come from?'

'I know very little. He came to Australia to seek his fortune. He must have come from a wealthy family because he bought the land your house is currently on, plus about twenty acres. He was a farmer for a while, but not a very good one. He wasn't a young man when he married. I think he was in his mid to late forties. My father said once that he always seemed old to him. He was a quiet man who kept himself to himself. The acres are gone now, of course, your grandfather sold most of the acreage off, as the area built up many years ago.'

'Do you have any old papers of his?'

'No. I do have a few photos, but not much else. If there are any old documents, you'll probably find them in the attic at your place.'

'Of course. I didn't think to look up there.'

'What's going on?'

Jubilee hesitated for a moment. 'I found something buried in the back garden. I'm trying to trace where it came from and who put it there.'

'Sounds intriguing. What?'

'Ah … I'd rather not say now. I want to do a little more research first. I'll fill you in later, if that's okay.'

'Sure, sweetie. But be careful. As your Nana used to say, "nothing good ever comes from digging up the past".'

Jubilee began to laugh. Her mother had often used the same quote.

'I will. Thanks Aunt Joan.'

After they finished their drinks, Joan took Jubilee inside and pulled out her old family photo albums. She found a picture of Jack Jones on his wedding day in 1942. Jubilee looked long and hard at the black and white photo. She had never seen a picture of her great-grandfather until now. However, the man standing beside his expressionless wife was the same man she saw in the passport photo the previous week. Although, the name stated Jack Hawthorn – not Jack Jones. She took a photo of the wedding picture on her mobile. Then thanking her aunt, she left, promising to come to dinner on Sunday.

Joan watched as Jubilee walked back to her car. She had promised her sister, Mauve that she would keep an eye on Jubilee whilst she was in Mackay. Jubilee had been distant since her return to Bowral. The sisters had decided to give Jubilee some time and space to sort herself out. Although her niece was thirty-two, and a confident woman, Joan had witnessed Jubilee's inhibited behaviour on a few occasions. As Mauve had decided to stay in Mackay, Joan was only too happy to keep an eye on Jubilee on her sister's behalf.

Back in her car, Jubilee sat and stared at the wedding photo of Jack Jones.

'Who the hell are you? Was it you that buried all that jewellery? Did you steal it?' Jubilee was becoming more intrigued with this new turn of events. It only made her more determined to uncover the truth.

As soon as Jubilee arrived home, she headed straight up into the attic and spent an hour rummaging through decades of old boxes until she found what she was looking for. Underneath a canvas tarpaulin was a wooden chest. Inside the chest was an array of old photos, documents, and memorabilia. On her knees, Jubilee scrutinised every item, but they revealed nothing about who Jack Jones was prior to his arrival in Australia. It was as if he didn't exist.

There wasn't much to show for Jack Jones' life. He could have passed through life unnoticed or forgotten. That thought left Jubilee feeling depressed.

However, at the bottom of the chest was a locked box. Jubilee carried it downstairs and broke the lock with a crowbar. Inside was a man's neck scarf. It was knitted and obviously handmade. There was also a man's wallet. It had the initials J. H. embedded on the front in gold leaf foil. The wallet was empty, except for a letter. It read:

My dear Mary,

You've been a good wife. Kept me on the straight and narrow.

I didn't deserve you.

You wanted nothing to do with my past. Fair to ya. But if you ever change your mind look for the key where you always threatened to send me, it's hanging in plain sight.

Do with it as you will. You already know where the tin is buried.

Trust no one.

Your humble servant, Jack

Jubilee couldn't believe what she just read.

'What key?' she said out loud to the empty room.

Jubilee retrieved the photo she found with the passport and looked at the happy family. Were they Jack's family? He wasn't in the photo. She picked up the handmade scarf and examined it. It was knitted in royal blue wool, with a white and red stripe criss-crossing down the scarf. *J.H.* was sewn into a handmade label at one end, *With Love, M.H.* below it.

Who was M.H.?

Another question for Aunt Joan on Sunday.

Jubilee sat by the fireplace with a glass of red, re-reading the short note again and again: *look for the key where you always threatened to send me.* Where do people go when they're bad, she wondered? Jail, their bedroom, the naughty corner, she mused.

Jubilee decided to fill her aunt in on everything she had discovered at dinner on Sunday. She'd know what to do.

Chapter Four

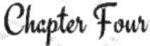

Mittagong

June 18 – Sunday lunch

Present at Sunday lunch was Jubilee's Uncle Phil and her aunt, and two of her cousins, Meg and Jodie. Emily, the youngest, worked in Canberra and couldn't visit that weekend. During a delicious lamb roast, Jubilee revealed her secret about Jack Jones and what she'd dug up in the back garden.

All four were gobsmacked while they listened to Jubilee's story. Traditionally, her Uncle Phil would have already been in the kitchen doing the dishes by then, except everyone was too engrossed in the story to leave the table.

'Have you authenticated the jewellery yet, in case they're fake?' Meg asked, still finding it hard to believe what her cousin had told them.

'No. I've been too afraid to remove them from my wardrobe.' Joan chuckled at her niece's caginess.

'How did your search go in the attic, Jubilee?' Joan asked.

'I found some old photos and a wallet in a locked box. But there was also a passport and photo in the biscuit tin. Hang on a minute.' Jubilee jumped up and retrieved her handbag from the living room. On her return, she handed Joan the passport and photo, plus the letter she found in the wallet.

'Do you recognise anyone in that photo?'

Joan studied the photo for some time but reluctantly said she didn't. On the back she read the inscription, *Hawthorn Manor, March, 1939* and the small note in the bottom corner, *1948 CBBBS*. Then she read the letter but finished with a puzzled expression on her face.

She handed the letter back to Jubilee and said, 'Maybe you should ask your grandmother about this. It may make sense to her, if she's able to remember.'

Jubilee felt instantly ashamed; she hadn't visited her grandmother for weeks. She'd been too caught up in her own melodrama to think how her grandmother was faring. Jubilee agreed to go and see her in the next few days.

'I want to find out who owned this jewellery and if the family in this picture is Jack's. How do I go about that?'

'Look at Ancestry, the website,' Meg said. 'You can trace Jack's ancestors. But you should verify if the jewellery is genuine, Jubes, otherwise you're just wasting your time.' Meg had always called her cousin Jubes since they were children, after her favourite sweets. They were only four months apart in age and had been inseparable during their childhood. Meg owned an antique bookshop in Bowral, so when Jubilee headed to Sydney to begin her apprenticeship and study commercial cookery, they saw less and less of each other. Since her return, Meg had been a lifeline for Jubilee and their friendship had rebounded.

'How?' Jubilee asked.

'Each piece of jewellery will have symbols etched on them somewhere,' Meg continued. 'There would be gold and silver markings, sometimes the year they were made. There could be the jeweller's trademark. You could Google them, there's bound to be a site somewhere. Then, you can trace who they belonged to through the jeweller, if they're still around, that is. If not, you could try auction houses like Christie's or Sotheby's.'

'Thanks Meg, but what if he stole them? His passport said Jack Hawthorn not Jack Jones. Why would he change his name?'

'I'd say he stole the passport, Jubilee,' her uncle interjected.

'Even more reason to be suspicious,' Jubilee added. 'Meg, would you help me trace Jack's family and the jewellers so we can identify the actual owners.'

'Why not? It sounds fascinating. I'll come over tomorrow night. I'm already registered on Ancestry. I was searching Dad's family for him. I can easily create a search for Mum's side as well. I've also got a magnifying glass at work, which I'll bring with me so we can identify the jeweller's trademark.'

Jubilee felt like she was getting somewhere, now that Meg was on board.

'One more thing, Jubilee,' her uncle sounded concerned, the lawyer in him taking over. 'You should contact the police and tell them what you've found. As you're trying to trace the owners, the police will expect you to document and record everything you discover.'

'Why? I know I can't keep them,' Jubilee stated.

'Phil's right, Jubilee,' Joan said flatly.

'You need to be careful,' he continued. 'If you want to discover who owned these jewels, that's all very well and good, but you must make sure you hand them over to the right descendants, and that will require police assistance. Whoever owned them might have willed them to a particular person, not necessarily a direct descendant. The police will have more resources than you, including contacts to robbery units in the UK, if that's where they originated from.'

For the first time, Jubilee realised how profoundly complex her situation was. It was becoming very real. Her uncle was right, of course.

Meg could sense Jubilee's apprehension about going to the police, but listening to her cousin over lunch, she could see Jubilee was finally passionate about something, so she offered up an alternative scenario. 'Look, why don't I pop into the local police station in Bowral during my lunch break tomorrow? I'll make discreet enquiries regarding your situation and see what we are required to do legally. That way I won't be directly naming you, Jubes.'

After a moment's hesitation, Jubilee nodded her agreement. Jubilee and Meg formulated a plan. After a nightcap, Jubilee headed home and waited eagerly for the following evening.

*   *   *

Jubilee retrieved the Arnott's biscuit tin from the back of the wardrobe and placed it gently on her bed. She strained to see any symbols on the backs of the jewellery pieces. She found some tiny markings on the inside of the rings, but she squinted so hard she gave herself a headache. She decided to wait until Meg arrived tomorrow with her magnifying glass.

Jubilee placed the jewels neatly on the velvet cloth before putting them to bed for the night, unintentionally, smiling down at them.

They twinkled back at her.

Chapter Five

Bowral Police Station

June 19 – Monday lunchtime

True to her word, Meg arrived at the Bowral Police Station a little after one in the afternoon. She had thought all morning about what she was going to say, but as she walked inside, she became anxious. Meg asked herself, what would Miss Marple do? Probably, she would come across as all sweet and innocent in order to put her suspect off their guard whilst she matter-of-factly knitted a jumper as a distraction. Meg didn't know how to knit, and as she approached the front desk, her confidence waned.

A young female police constable looked up at her and smiled. Meg looked around the room. There was a middle-aged man reading something on his mobile as his leg tapped away vigorously, and a teenager who was biting his nails and twitching nervously.

'How can I help you?' she asked politely.

'I would like to speak to someone about stolen property,' Meg said, before adding, 'allegedly.'

'Was it stolen or not?' she asked, a little less politely.

'I'm not sure.'

'Can't you find it?'

Meg was puzzled!

'Oh no, I mean I found something but I'm not sure if it was stolen or just lost and found. I wanted to ask about the legal responsibilities. I just don't know if it was stolen or not ... yet.'

'Right! I see,' the constable said with a little more enthusiasm. 'In that case, you can simply hand it in and we'll do everything we can to find the owner. They may have lodged a claim with us. When did you find it?'

'A week ago. But it may have been buried for over fifty years,' Meg said, with a wry smile.

'What?'

'It was found buried in a back garden. I don't know if a family member buried it and forgot about it, or if they stole it and put it there for safe keeping.'

'I see,' the constable nodded, taking a closer look at Meg.

'I want to know if I can search for the owner myself, and if there are any legal requirements.'

'Well, you can hand it in to us, as I said before, as we have more resources than you to locate the owner. I'll get a sergeant to come out and talk to you if you want to know your legal rights.'

'Thank you.'

The constable asked Meg to take a seat while she placed a call and spoke quietly into the telephone. Meg sat next to the twitching teenager. She wondered if the twitchiness had something to do with the building they were currently in. Meg realised that anything said in this station could be taken down and used against you in a court of law. She started to twitch.

Meg didn't have to wait long before a thirty-something year old man walked through a door and toward the constable who nodded in Meg's direction.

As he approached her, he paused for a moment and studied her, then he extended his hand and introduced himself as Sergeant Billy Banker. Meg raised her hand and introduced herself, thinking how confusing it must be for a banker to be a policeman. She tried hard not to make a joke of it in case he didn't have a sense of humour.

'Meg Forrester,' she said, biting her lip.

'Please come with me.'

Meg followed the sergeant to the same door, which he opened after swiping his security card. He stood aside for Meg to enter and followed behind her. He showed her to an interview room, which felt very intimidating. He asked her if she would like a cup of tea or coffee. Meg politely declined. Miss Marple had vanished. Meg felt completely alone. She should have asked her dad to accompany her.

'If I heard the constable correctly, you were enquiring about stolen property?' he asked, smiling.

'Yes and No,' she began. 'I don't know yet that the property was stolen, which is why I'm here to find out what legal ramifications there are for me if I investigate where they came from and who owned them.'

'I see,' he said.

Meg was beginning to wonder if all police say 'I see' when they're unsure. He only smiled at her again, which began to annoy her.

'Sorry, but do I have egg on my face, or ink maybe, as you seem to think this is comical.'

Sergeant Banker blushed a little and apologised. 'I'm sorry, but I know you. You work in the bookshop in town, don't you?'

'Well, yes, I do. I own it actually.'

'I thought so. I recognised you when I popped in there last month to buy the latest Matthew Riley novel.'

Awkward moment, Meg thought. She wasn't expecting that. So much for controlling the narrative.

As if he read her mind, he said, 'It's okay. I probably wouldn't remember me either. I'm from here actually. My parents divorced many years ago and I moved away with my mum. I transferred back to Bowral after I became a sergeant, which was about a year ago. Anyway, what do you want to know?'

Meg sighed with relief. 'I want to know if I'm allowed to search for the owner of the jewellery myself. Or do I have to hand it in to you straight away?'

'Jewellery!'

Meg swore under her breath as she let slip what was found. She reminded herself to be more guarded next time.

'Well … There's no urgency to hand them in straight away, as long as you document everything you've found. You need to time and date every page and state the place they were found and by whom. Take photographs including where you found it and if it was wrapped in anything. Chances are, you will only have limited access to information, whereas the police will have far more resources including contacts to robbery units in and around Australia, and overseas if necessary.'

'Right. Thank you,' Meg said.

'Why can't you just hand it in?'

'Because there's a story behind it, and I think it's worth telling.'

Sergeant Banker nodded his understanding. 'You can investigate further yourself, but returning the jewellery to the owner, could pose a risk if you don't hand the jewellery over to the rightful legal owner. The police are in a better position to find the legal owner or owners through probate and the courts.'

Meg was thoughtful for a moment.

'How many pieces of jewellery have you found?'

Meg was reluctant to say anymore.

'There is no statute of limitations regarding robbery, so there may be a crime to investigate.'

'Oh no. These jewels have been buried for decades, maybe as far back as the 1940s. If they were stolen, it may have happened in England.'

'We have an extradition treaty with England, but if they were stolen that long ago, of course, no one would be alive today to prosecute, but finding the owners would be more complicated.'

'What if I put them in the bank for safekeeping while I try to locate the owners? If I can't find them, I can hand the jewellery over to the police. But if I do find the owners, I'll verify with you before handing anything over. Would that work?'

'Yes. Just make sure to document everything as you go along. If you hit a snag, contact me and I'll help you. If we cannot locate the owners, you can then lodge a claim to keep them. But there's no such thing as 'finder's keepers', you must make every attempt to locate the owners.'

For a moment, Meg was surprised she hadn't thought about Jubilee keeping the jewellery. She had a lot to think about. Meg thanked Sergeant Banker for his help.

'Look … Begin your search and see how you get on. I'm here if you need me. Are the jewels very valuable?'

'I think so.'

'Okay, record everything, then send me copies as a backup and I'll open up a case file and assist you.'

'Thanks again, Sergeant Banker. You've been very helpful.'

'My pleasure, and please call me Billy – just not Willy,' he said giving her a sly look. He stood up and shook Meg's hand once more.

'Then you can call me Meg,' she said, all the while thinking, *why on Earth would I call him Willy?*

Meg was escorted out towards the reception area, she now felt more relaxed knowing what Jubilee needed to do. She passed the twitching boy, who had started biting his other hand's nails, and gave him a wink of reassurance on her way out.

Meg walked back to her shop, her thoughts briefly flickering back to Sergeant Billy Banker. He seemed helpful enough, though a little odd. At least he was a book reader of the paperback kind. Meg called Jubilee and updated her on what the police sergeant had said. Jubilee agreed and said she would start photographing and documenting everything, including a timeline of her investigation.

*   *   *

A little after 6:00 pm, Meg arrived at Jubilee's home with a bottle of wine. It went down well with the delicious crab and mushroom risotto Jubilee had made. When the wine bottle had mysteriously emptied, they cleared the dining room table and Jubilee fetched the Arnott's biscuit tin.

Meg had retrieved her magnifying glass as Jubilee re-entered the room.

Jubilee opened the tin and removed the velvet cloth. She enjoyed the expression on Meg's face when she revealed what was inside. Although Jubilee had become accustomed to their elegance and beauty, Meg was in disbelief. Jubilee gave her cousin a minute to recover. Meg tried on the emerald necklace. It was heavier than it looked draped around her neck. The jewel emanated sophistication and elegance. It accentuated Meg's black, off-the-shoulder straight hair and green eyes. Jubilee surmised that the artist knew exactly what they were doing when they designed it.

'How do I look?' Meg asked.

'Like a million dollars.' They both laughed. The emeralds sparkled under the lights in the dining room, proud to be on display again.

Each piece of jewellery was placed on the dining table. Jubilee had taken photos of each piece of jewellery and printed the image on her laser printer. Meg picked up the first item – a ring. Then, using the magnifying glass, she wrote on the printout the symbols that appeared on the inside gold band.

Pieces that were clearly part of a set, they kept together. The magnificent ruby necklace, bracelet, earrings and ring stood out above all others. The set was intricately designed with diamond clusters surrounding each ruby to accentuate its beauty. The largest ruby of them all was the centrepiece of the necklace. Meg surmised this particular stone would have to be recorded somewhere in the jewellery trade, because of its size. She then traced a repeating symbol on all four pieces of jewellery, signifying the jeweller who made them. The other symbols denoted the gold and silver markings and the year the jewellery was made – 1939.

'Well, at least we know they couldn't have been stolen any earlier than 1939,' Jubilee declared.

'Agreed. It now gives us a time frame to work with,' Meg added.

When Meg finished documenting all the symbols, Jubilee started to search on the internet for jewellers' trademarks. It was proving to be very difficult, so she decided to put that idea aside and personally visit a local jeweller in Bowral in the morning and see if they could help her identify the trademark symbols. Jubilee decided to help Meg tackle Ancestry and see what they could find out about their great-grandfather, Jack Jones.

Meg told Jubilee what she was looking for. 'We can find out through the Australian National Archives which ship he arrived on. We just have to search using his name. We'll search under Jack Hawthorn first, as that was the name on the passport, plus it had a customs stamp and arrival date for Sydney, Australia.'

Meg brought up the Australian shipping and passenger records and searched for Jack Hawthorn. They scanned down the list until they found his name.

'Oh wow! There he is!' Jubilee was excited. 'That must be him.'

Meg picked up the photo that Jubilee found in the passport and turned it over. The date on the back said March 1939, and the dress style fitted that decade. Meg looked up Hawthorn Manor online. It was in St Ives, Cornwall, and was now a five-star hotel. Digging into the family history, the Hawthorn family had lived there for over 350 years. Jack Hawthorn was the second son of Robert and Eleanor Hawthorn. Their four children were Stewart, Margaret, Jack, and Elizabeth.

'This must be his family. M.H. must be Margaret,' Jubilee said, excitedly, reminding Meg about the label on the knitted scarf. It was starting to get very real and personal with each new search they instigated.

'Holy shit!' Meg uttered, under her breath. 'If Jack Hawthorn is in this picture, it isn't our great-grandfather. He looks nothing like him.'

Jubilee agreed, but they needed to be sure.

'Your dad said he probably stole this man's passport?' Jubilee said tapping her finger on the passport photo.

'Being a jewel thief would be a good reason,' Meg replied flippantly.

'Do you think he stole from them?' Jubilee asked, holding the photograph of the Hawthorn family.

'Let's find out.' Meg started typing.

'What if he was the black sheep of the family?' Jubilee added. 'That's why he's not in the picture and then he changed his name after he arrived.'

'Jubes, you can't make him good if he was a bad egg.'

'But if he did steal this jewellery why hasn't anyone come looking? They're clearly valuable.'

'Well, September 1939 was the beginning of World War Two. Maybe after six years of fighting the authorities had forgotten about it. Or there wasn't enough manpower and resources to re-open the investigation.'

'How awful. To be lost in time like that.'

Meg could see her cousin was becoming nostalgic. A romantic habit she always mastered well but which never did her any favours. Sentimentality wasn't very practical right now.

Jubilee came back to earth. 'We can check newspapers and the local churches as well as the births, deaths, and marriages registries.'

'Absolutely. There are many avenues to go down.'

'Thanks for helping, Meg. I never would have gotten this far without you.' Jubilee didn't have a Facebook account, or any other platform for socialising, for the simple reason that she wouldn't have the patience to maintain it.

'Anytime. I'm rather enjoying myself. I can't come tomorrow night, but I'll come over after work on Wednesday, and we can search some more. Now I've got to go to bed, I'm dead tired and I've got a shipment of books coming in the morning.'

Jubilee hadn't realised how late it had become. 'Oh shit! Sorry Meg. Why don't you sleep in the spare room tonight? I'll make you breakfast before you head out.'

'Why not,' Meg said, never turning down an offer of a meal cooked by Jubilee.

'Have you dated and recorded everything so far, as Sergeant Banker suggested?'

'Yes, I started after you called me. Why does that name sound familiar? What was his first name again?'

'Billy. Why?'

'That's it! Don't you remember, he painted all over the back of your uniform in art class back in third grade and you punched him on the nose? You called him Wanker after that, Willy Wanker.'

'Oh my god! That was him!' exclaimed Meg, after a flash-bulb moment. Now she understood Billy's behaviour back at the police station.

'Just don't call him that now for god's sake, we're going to need his help.'

Meg could only cringe.

Jubilee packed up the jewellery and tucked them in for the night, but she couldn't sleep, she had too much history roaming around inside her head to settle. She lay awake thinking about what she needed to do next.

Jubilee hoped Jack hadn't stolen the jewellery from his own family. She was just getting to know him and wanted to like him. She had also decided to visit her Nan tomorrow. The nursing home was open again to visitors, but it was her Nan's memory that concerned Jubilee. Hopefully, her Nan could shed some light on her father-in-law, Jack Jones. Would she even remember Jubilee tomorrow? She was coherent most days, but on other days, her family were strangers to her.

Jubilee decided to make her Nan a lemon meringue pie. It was her favourite.

She hoped she'd remember that!

Chapter Six

Jubilee's House, Bowral

June 20 – Tuesday morning

Jubilee made Meg poached eggs on toast before sending her on her way. She was too excited to wait until Meg returned to continue her research, so she opened her laptop and tried again to search for jeweller trademarks.

This morning, she had more luck. Pinterest revealed images, but she couldn't find any remotely similar to the images Meg had drawn. Later, Jubilee found a website that had everything she needed to know about jeweller trademarks. She poured herself a coffee and settled in for a long read, making extensive notes as she went.

By the time Jubilee finished reading, she was confident the jewellery was genuine as the karat of gold recorded on the jewellery was between eighteen and twenty-four. If the gold and silver markings were to be believed, then the stones had to also be real. She decided to take one pair of earrings to a jeweller in Bowral and ask for an evaluation. She needed to know one way or another. First, she had a lemon meringue pie to make.

*   *   *

Once Jubilee had signed herself in at the aged care home she headed to her grandmother's room. The last few years had been hard for her grandmother. The aged care home had been closed to visitors when COVID was at its worst. Mauve and Joan had been concerned that their mother's mental health would deteriorate more rapidly without frequent visits from her family. The only way they could converse with her was on Zoom or Messenger. They had been indebted to the aged care workers, who arranged times for Mauve and Joan to talk to their mother on an iPad.

When Jubilee entered her grandmother's room, she found her sitting in a chair gazing out the window at the beautiful Bowral countryside. There had been substantial rain over the last few years and the countryside was greener than Jubilee had ever seen it. Sarah Jones had a book open on her lap. Meg would bring her grandmother a new book from her bookshop each week, but Jubilee wondered how many times she had read the same page. Her heart went out to her.

'Hi, Nan,' Jubilee said as she leaned down and kissed her on the cheek. She then put the lemon meringue pie on the side table.

Her grandmother looked at her but didn't recognise her. Jubilee knew the routine: just keep talking to her and hopefully it will trigger a memory.

She held a one-way conversation for nearly twenty minutes before her grandmother finally turned to Jubilee with a look of recognition in her eyes.

'Hello, Jubilee,' she said in a soft voice.

'Welcome back,' she replied. 'Your hair looks nice today.'

'Yes. A hairdresser came in yesterday and styled it for me. She comes once a week. Nice girl. Although, this time it needed a cut. It had grown quite long.'

'I liked it long. You could pin it back into a bun.'

'Yes. That's right.' Sarah Jones turned back to the window.

'I was hoping to test your memory today. I want to ask you about your father-in-law, Jack Jones.'

Sarah's expression changed. 'Why do you want to know about him?'

'I'm researching our family background and he appears to be a bit of a mystery.'

'Let sleeping dogs lie, Jubilee,' Sarah said, with finality. She turned away from her granddaughter and continued to enjoy the view.

'I can't, Nan. Please ... something has happened. I need to know everything I can about him. Meg is helping me but we need you to fill in the blanks.'

Sarah turned back to her granddaughter. She seemed to drift for a moment. Jubilee hoped her memory wasn't disappearing again so quickly.

Sarah wondered how much she should tell her granddaughter about Jack Jones. She knew no good would come of it, but he died long ago, so what would it matter now? Sarah decided to confide in Jubilee.

'He was a quiet and guarded man. I learned not to ask too many questions. Michael, your granddad, was a gentle soul like his mother Mary, but Jack had a dark side. I first thought it was due to the war, but he never served. At times, he was a cold and unemotional man.'

'Do you know how he made his money? How he was able to buy the land our house is on?'

'That's right … he bought the land but I never knew where the money came from. It wasn't from Mary's side of the family and he never spoke about his. Mary said once that he was a complicated man, but she loved him. He treated her well and he was a good father to Michael. But you could never ask him about his past.'

'Do you recall hearing anything about a place called Hawthorn Manor in Cornwall, England?'

There was a short pause. 'No … Why do you ask?'

'I think that's where he came from, and I think he may have stolen something before he arrived in Australia.'

Sarah was thoughtful for a moment. Her fractured mind was searching for a recollection.

'I remember one day I was sitting at the table writing letters to my family. I asked him if he ever wrote to his family back in England. He said they were all dead. I asked him where he was from. He said London and said no more than that.'

'So, you knew he emigrated from England?'

Sarah chuckled. 'His accent gave that away.'

'Did he ever give the impression that he wasn't who he claimed to be?'

Sarah eyed her granddaughter.

Jubilee could see her grandmother was growing sceptical about the questions she was asking. But her grandmother was thoughtful as another memory stirred.

'I think your great-grandmother knew something about his past. One day I returned home from town when I heard them arguing in the kitchen. I was outside the door and dared not enter while they fought. She said something like, "I don't want to know where it came from. No good will come of it. Do you want to be hanged?" I never found out what she was talking about. I was too afraid to ask. Once they stopped arguing, I entered the room and it was as if the conversation never took place.'

Jubilee's face glowed with intrigue. She leaned a little closer to her grandmother and allowed her to continue at her own pace.

'Your great-grandfather had a stroke – a bad one. Michael sat with him during his last days. His words slurred at the end, leaving him agitated and frustrated. Michael said he spoke about Jews and betrayals, something to that effect. Mary told Michael not to take anything his father said seriously because he was confused. But Michael stayed by his side until he died. He later told me that his father kept mumbling about not selling the house. Michael promised him he wouldn't. But over the years he did sell off the last of the acreage when he needed money. But he never sold the house.'

'Did he ever tell you why not?'

'No.'

'Thank you, Nan. You've been a great help.'

Jubilee read her grandmother the letter that Jack had left for Mary. She asked if the final part meant anything to her. Her grandmother giggled.

'When he drank he could be vulgar,' she said. 'Mary often threatened to make him sleep with his dog. Oh … what was his name? Finn … that's it. Jack often said that he had no greater trusted friend.'

Jubilee took her grandmother for a stroll in the gardens. They talked a little more about Jack Jones, but when they returned her grandmother seemed tired and hadn't spoken in a while.

Jubilee made her grandmother comfortable in the chair by the window. Looking up at her granddaughter she said, 'I'm so glad you came Mauve, I've missed you.'

Jubilee wanted to cry. 'It's me, Nan. It's Jubilee.'

Slowly, Sarah Jones appeared to drift back into her own private world, which didn't include her family. Jubilee cut her a slice of lemon meringue pie and kissed her on the forehead before leaving.

Chapter Seven

Bowral Town Centre

June 20 – Tuesday afternoon

Jubilee headed into Bowral's town centre in search of a jeweller. She wrapped her 'new' scarf around her neck to keep the chilly June wind off her chest as she walked along the busy street. It wasn't actually new; it was the scarf she found in the attic – delicately washed three times to get the stuffy old smell out of it. Wearing it made her feel nostalgic and a part of Jack's history.

Jubilee entered the shop and asked the sales assistant if she could speak with the jeweller. The young woman went into the back of the shop and returned moments later, followed by an older woman in her fifties who introduced herself as the jeweller.

'How can I help you?' she asked.

'I was hoping you could take a look at a pair of earrings and tell me if they're authentic pearls and if you can identify the trademark on the back?'

Jubilee handed over an old earring box. The jeweller opened it to reveal a set of pearl earrings.

The woman examined them closely using a jeweller's loupe, which magnified the symbols at least ten times their true size.

The pearls hung below a cluster of five diamonds, which were inlaid in a square pattern. One diamond for each corner and one larger one in the centre.

'They are magnificent,' she said.

'What can you tell me about them?'

'These are golden South Sea pearls. They are the most expensive pearls in the world and considering their size, two of the largest I've seen up close. The diamonds are flawless and inlaid in eighteen karat white gold. The entire piece is exquisite. Are they a family heirloom?'

'Yes. I think they are over 100 years old.'

'That, they are. The year 1852 is next to the karat engraving. Do you want to sell them?'

'No!' Jubilee replied a little too quickly. 'They've been in my family a long time. I just want to know, for insurance purposes, their current value.'

'I can only give you an estimate. But I would humbly say these earrings could fetch at auction around $40,000 to $50,000.'

'What?'

'It's the craftsmanship and also the quality of the pearls and diamonds. The symbol on the back of the earrings means the diamonds are flawless. Here, take a look!'

The jeweller handed Jubilee her loupe so she could see the symbol for herself. It stated *FL*.

'However, my evaluation is only an estimate. If you do decide to sell them, an auction house would be your best bet. I'm sure you'll have buyers bidding as high as $50,000 if not more. That is U.S. dollars, by the way.'

Jubilee was gobsmacked; she could only imagine the value of the other pieces of jewellery inside her biscuit tin if this was anything to go by.

'Do you recognise the jeweller who made them? I wanted to contact them.'

'It isn't one I recognise. Though, I think I may still have an old book of jeweller trademarks somewhere in the back. I can lend it to you if it's important to you, I rarely use it.'

'Thank you. That would be very helpful. I'll return it as soon as I'm finished.'

The jeweller went into the back of the shop to retrieve the old handbook. Jubilee was pleased with herself, now she could potentially identify the jewellers for many of her pieces and contact them. That's if they were still in business and were willing to talk to her. If they refused to help, Sergeant Banker would be her next contact. That thought reminded her of Meg, which made her laugh.

After leaving the jewellery shop, Jubilee took a stroll through town. She felt like her life had just taken a mischievous but exhilarating turn for the better. She was on the verge of something new and exciting, thrilling wouldn't be an understatement. All she knew for sure was a week ago, she was feeling morose and sorry for herself, but now she had a purpose and more importantly, she had adrenalin in her bones. Something was brewing in the frisky Bowral fresh air.

She passed a cafe and decided to treat herself and Meg to a coffee and cake. She wanted to tell Meg her good news in person. As she entered the shop, she noticed a dog sitting by its owner's side at one of the outside tables and was reminded of something that her grandmother had said, 'Mary often threatened to send Jack to the doghouse'. Jubilee remembered that she had knocked down a doghouse over a week ago and dumped it in a skip.

Quick as a flash, Jubilee ran back to her car. Dodging past people on the pavement and apologising profusely as she did, she raced home, and after changing her shoes, she dug up the soil around where the doghouse had once resided. But found nothing. She walked over to the skip and looked inside. She knew she'd have to go in. She cringed, then thought, *In for a penny, in for a pound*, and climbed into the skip. She delicately rummaged around until she retrieved what was left of the doghouse.

Jubilee placed each piece on the ground and studied it, but the slats of old rotten wood revealed nothing. She knew the note implied something important. The doghouse was significant in some way.

Hanging from a crossbeam was an old broken chain, but there was nothing on the end of it. She wondered what had been there. Then she remembered the squeaky toy she dug up the previous week. She raced back to the skip and climbed in again. Carefully, she fumbled through the skip until she found the old rubber toy in the shape of a bone. Jubilee squeezed it, but it only made a sad whinging sound. That is until she shook it when it rattled. Something was inside it.

Jubilee used a pair of hedge cutters and cut into the rubber bone. Out dropped a key. A large bronze key.

'What the hell!' she exclaimed. Why would Jack Jones put a key in a rubber dog bone?

It didn't look like your average door key.

'Well, you have to unlock something!' she said. She moved around the house and garden to see if it fitted any of the locks. But nothing came close.

Since the biscuit tin had no lock on it, Jubilee wasn't sure what the key opened. She put the key in the tin along with the wallet and passport. Tomorrow, she would figure out what it opened, because today she wanted to check the jeweller's handbook for trademarks.

By the time she went to bed at midnight, she had identified four jewellers, including the karat and the year made.

Chapter Eight

Jubilee's House, Bowral

June 21 – Wednesday morning

Jubilee was up early and back at her computer before the coffee finished brewing. She searched the internet for the four jewellers she'd identified the night before and discovered three were still registered and working in Hatton Garden, London, England.

Once Jubilee was sure she had the correct jewellers she checked the time – it was now 9:30 am. She couldn't call them as she was nine hours ahead of England, making it roughly midnight in London. She decided to send emails as it would be easier to say what she wanted rather than blurting out too much too soon. She didn't trust herself to be discreet.

She found the email address for Lieberman and Bach, fine jewellers since 1795, and sent her first message.

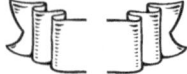

Dear Sir/Madam,

I'm hoping you can help me trace the owners of the jewellery shown in the attached photos. Golden South Sea pearl earrings (1852) and an emerald necklace, with matching bracelet and ring (1870) that were made by your company. For your consideration, I have also included images of the symbols imprinted on the jewellery. I know it is an unusual request, but I was hoping your records would identify who they were commissioned for.

Any information you can provide would be greatly appreciated.

Yours sincerely,

Jubilee Jones.

Jubilee paused before hitting the send button. Was she being naïve? Once she hit send, there was no going back. If they knew anything, would they refuse to help, stating privacy laws? Or would they contact the police? Jubilee had only one option if she wanted answers. She hit the send button. Then she sent an email to the second jeweller on her list, Starr and Everett. This time, she attached a picture of a diamond necklace and matching earrings but decided not to mention the ruby set. Strangely, she felt overly protective of the rubies and didn't want to reveal their current whereabouts.

Jubilee had never appreciated the beauty of jewellery until she opened that biscuit tin. She was never one for accessorising. Her usual attire consisted of a watch her mother gave her for Christmas a few years ago, a pair of gold studded earrings which were only replaced when one went missing, and the ring her grandmother gave her on her 21st birthday.

Now, the artist in her appreciated the architecture and skill that went into designing each piece of jewellery. Working at The Mariner, she had created five-star menus that pleased and delighted her customers, who came back to dine repeatedly.

The world would always need artists, she thought.

Jubilee's final email was to Blackman and Chambers. Even though they were no longer fine jewellers, their website stated they were diamond traders. She sent attachments of a diamond ring with blue stones surrounding it. Jubilee wasn't sure if they were sapphires, lapis lazuli, or topaz. The fourth jeweller on Jubilee's list was harder to trace. She couldn't find them listed anywhere and had to assume they were no longer operating. Jubilee still had seven pieces of jewellery to identify. She hoped the jewellers wouldn't ask too many questions yet grew concerned they wouldn't even bother to reply.

*   *   *

When Meg arrived after work, Jubilee filled her in on what their grandmother had said. Meg was puzzled by the reference to Jews and betrayals. Her family weren't anti-Semitic, far from it.

'I think she misheard,' Meg said. 'It could be *jewels*, not *Jews*.'

'Of course,' Jubilee said, raising her eyebrows to the sky.

Then Jubilee showed Meg the key she found hidden in the toy dog bone. Meg was dumbfounded.

'Who the hell hides a key in a toy dog bone? It's like something out of a Sherlock Holmes novel.'

Jubilee could only shake her head.

Meg opened up her computer and searched Ancestry to see if they had any links. She explained to Jubilee what she was looking for. The website provided access to vast collections of records, such as census data, birth, death and marriage certificates, and user-contributed family trees. Through its data matching algorithms, users could discover relatives and build their own family trees online. So far, she hadn't had much to go on and London covered a lot of ground. Worst of all, Jones was a common name and probably not his real name.

Meg was disappointed as their searches would take time and probably reveal very little.

'Maybe he lied to Nan. Maybe he wasn't from London at all,' Meg said. 'There are other British ancestry websites we could search like My Heritage, and Find My Past, but we could hit the same roadblocks. We could also try newspapers and census records,' she said, still trying to be positive. 'In England, there's the British Newspaper Archive. We have to register, but it's for free. Then there's the British Library, it holds all newspaper records. Most of these will be on microfilm or microfiche. There's also a site called Google's News Archive. They may not have all the newspapers going back to the 1930s but we can check there. But our best bet is the National Archive in Kew, England.'

Jubilee was impressed her cousin had done a lot of homework.

Hours were wasted searching dead ends until she confirmed no Jack Jones had arrived in Australia in May, June or July 1939. They conceded it was a false name and a dead end. She would ask Billy to run a check on his name to make sure. Meg decided to bring up the website for the Hawthorn Hotel, previously known as Hawthorn Manor. After tracing the family history, they widened their search and found two obituaries. The first one Meg read was for the death of Eleanor Hawthorn, St Ives, Cornwall, in 1944. She died at home of a suspected heart attack. The second article related to the death of Jack Hawthorn, second son of Eleanor and Robert Hawthorn, St Ives, Cornwall, found dead in Plymouth in 1940.

Meg stopped in her tracks. She looked at Jubilee, who nodded that she should continue. 'His body was found in Plymouth a little under a year after his supposed departure for Australia. Police confirmed he had been stabbed. Council workers found his decayed body along with another unidentified man below street level in the sewer system. He was unrecognisable, but for his clothing, which contained a label with his name sewn onto it.'

'Holy shit, Jubes. What if our great-grandfather killed him and stole his passport then fled to Australia?'

'Oh, Meg. He's a killer too. But how did he know Jack Hawthorn?'

The cousins looked at each other in bewilderment.

'What other explanation could there be?'

Meg agreed. 'Why would Jack Hawthorn carry all that jewellery, unless he stole them from his own family? I mean, if he planned to leave England for Australia he would have bonds, cheques or cash, not jewellery. Maybe, he had nothing to do with the stolen jewellery at all.'

'How sad for Jack's family. They thought he left for Australia, only to discover he was killed and left to rot in a lousy sewer.'

Meg was shaking her head, 'If Jack kept a picture of the Hawthorn family with his passport, it must have some significance. It's incriminating.'

'God, I hope it wasn't a keepsake. Maybe he kept it out of guilt?'

No more words were needed. Meg found an email address on the hotel's contact website page, pleased that it was still owned by the Hawthorn family, and asked Jubilee to send them an email. The current owners were Susan and Henry Hawthorn. Hopefully, they could shed some light on what happened to Jack Hawthorn, the second son of Robert and Eleanor Hawthorn.

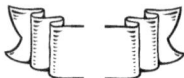

Dear Mr and Mrs Hawthorn,

My name is Jubilee Jones and I live in Australia. I was hoping you could help me with an inquiry regarding one of your ancestors.

I'm researching Jack Hawthorn, the second son of Robert and Eleanor Hawthorn. Supposedly departed for Sydney, Australia in May 1939, but was subsequently killed in Plymouth.

Any information you could shed on his death would be greatly appreciated.

I do not wish to cause your family any distress in revisiting the past, I only wish to discover the truth surrounding his death. I may be in a position to fill in some additional information.

I look forward to hearing from you.

Yours sincerely,

Jubilee Jones

It was now a waiting game.

Jubilee and Meg spent the rest of the evening trying to identify the remaining jewellery makers.

It was around 10:30 pm when Jubilee's email pinged her that she had a message.

It was from Henry Hawthorn. It read:

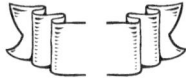

Dear Jubilee,

I was surprised but intrigued to receive your email. I do know certain details about Jack Hawthorn's death. I also checked our family records, which I'm not embarrassed to say have been dutifully well-maintained for over 400 years.

Jack Hawthorn left for Plymouth in May 1939. He had my great-grandfather's blessing to travel to Australia and make his own fortune through sheep farming. However, it wasn't until a year later that his family received news of his death. He never left Plymouth. He had been robbed and murdered. Scotland Yard believed whoever killed him, took his boarding pass and passport and travelled to Australia under his identity.

The Australian authorities confirmed a Jack Hawthorn arrived in Sydney on the *Jervis Bay*, but their investigations fell short of finding him. We can only assume the man changed his name and identity again on his arrival in Sydney.

We have my great-grandmother's journals that she wrote extensively during the year of Jack's disappearance. She feared something had happened to him as she hadn't received a letter, telegram or phone call from him since his supposed arrival in Sydney.

My great-grandmother died of a heart attack a few years after learning of his death. She was buried next to her son, Jack.

I also found some letters in her journal from the harbour master in Sydney and the Australian police to whom she must have written. They confirmed Jack's arrival but the Australian police could find no one using the name, Jack Hawthorn, after his arrival.

The police here in England hadn't discovered any new evidence, and with World War Two well underway, the investigation was put on hold. It was never re-opened. Eleanor Hawthorn hired a private detective to search for her son but the investigation revealed no new evidence, only conjecture.

May I ask why you are interested in Jack Hawthorn? Have you discovered something about his murder?

Yours respectfully,

Henry Hawthorn

'Holy shit!' exclaimed Meg.

'Then it's true.' Jubilee felt demoralised. 'He was a thief and a murderer.'

'We don't know that yet. Not for sure. Send a reply to Henry and ask him if he knows anything about stolen jewellery but ask delicately. And ask for a picture of Jack Hawthorn.'

Jubilee sent a reply.

Henry's reply arrived within the hour. Jubilee informed Meg that Henry knew nothing about any stolen jewellery and wanted to know why. He also asked if his great-uncle was involved in a crime. 'What should I say to him, Meg?'

'Reassure him that Jack Hawthorn isn't under suspicion for any crime and you've found his passport. Send him an image of the inside picture and the customs stamps and tell him you need more time to research what we have uncovered.'

Jubilee opened the attachment in Henry's last email. Both women looked at the picture of a young man, full of life, smiling back at a world ready to be explored. He looked confident and charming. This was not the man in her great-grandfather's wedding and passport photos. However, he was the same man in the photo Jubilee found with the old passport taken at Hawthorn Manor, along with his family in early 1939.

'I've got to find out, Meg. I have to know what happened. If Jack didn't steal them from Henry Hawthorn, then from who?'

'We will. It will take time. I think we should contact the National Archive in Kew. They have all of Scotland Yard's records. If this jewellery was stolen, they'd have a record of it. We should also check on the Australian side if there were any murders back in 1939. Maybe Jack murdered someone else on his arrival and took their identity, also.'

'Bloody hell!' exclaimed Jubilee. She remembered what her Aunt Joan had said about digging into the past.

'Look! We don't know anything yet. Don't forget – they found two bodies in the sewer. We don't know who the other body belonged to or what part they played in all this.'

Meg became quiet as she pondered the thought of two thieves entering Australia. Would the ancestors of the other man appreciate them snooping around and digging up the past?

Jubilee voiced her own idea that there could have been more than one thief and one betrayed the other before fleeing England.

Meg conceded that was possible, however, she reminded Jubilee not to jump to conclusions. 'I'll take Billy up on his offer and ask him to check the police archives to see if there were any unsolved murders around 1939 to 1940, and if there were any unsolved robberies in Australia at that time.'

Jubilee got up and proceeded to make them coffee. 'Well, you know what that means. Our surname is a lie. It isn't Jones at all. Who knows what it really is?'

When Jubilee returned to the kitchen table with the coffees, there was an email waiting for her from Lieberman and Bach.

'Oh, Meg, I've got a reply.'

'Quick. Read it.'

Both women leaned into the laptop as Jubilee read the reply.

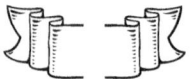

Dear Ms Jones,

Your email caught me off guard. The trademark is definitely ours. Did you take these photos from a book, or do you actually have these jewellery pieces?

I only ask because I found the purchase receipt in an archive box, dated 1852. They were made for one of our clients in the Cotswolds, near Cheltenham. A well-respected family near Bourton-on-the-Water. The commission was a gift for his wife on the birth of their first child.

I normally wouldn't give out this information, but I found a second document attached to the receipt. A letter from the police dated May 1939 pertaining to the theft of the earrings along with numerous other pieces of jewellery taken from their home on April 19, 1939.

Could I be so bold as to ask if you physically have this jewellery?

Yours respectfully,

Albert Bach.

'Holy crap!' exclaimed Meg.

'You said it.'

'Well, there's your proof, Jubes. If they're stolen, then the entire collection is stolen.'

'What do I do? Should I hand them to the police now or reply to Albert's email?'

Meg thought for a moment before answering, 'Don't give them to the police just yet. We still have time to trace the owners ourselves. Hopefully, we can discover the truth about Jack Jones, and who killed Jack Hawthorn. That's what you want, isn't it?'

Jubilee agreed with her cousin. It was far too personal now. Something deep inside her was yearning for the truth.

'You'll help me, won't you, Meg?'

'Of course I will. This is getting exciting. I feel like I'm in one of my mystery books. I'm itching to uncover our next clue.'

Jubilee held her cup up to her mouth, holding it in both hands. She twirled her ring absentmindedly as she contemplated her next move. Then she proclaimed, 'I think we need to go to England. That's where it all began. Waiting for email replies could take weeks. We have to be there in person to ask questions.'

Meg had a moment's hesitation as she had her bookshop to consider but then agreed. 'Why not! We can visit the National Archives in person. I'll organise for Jodie and Mum to run the bookshop while I'm away. We can hire a campervan; I've always wanted to travel around England in one of them. It'll be cheaper than B&Bs and hotels as my budget won't stretch that far. It'll be good to get away for a while, but I can only manage two weeks, though. I can't stay longer.'

'Then it's settled,' Jubilee said, with relief.

*   *   *

Jubilee updated her mother on the latest developments. Mauve was thrilled that Jubilee and Meg were heading to England. She hadn't heard this much excitement in her daughter's voice since she won a prestigious cooking award three years ago. Before saying goodnight, Mauve reiterated her earlier warning about opening up old wounds. 'They're hard to heal.'

'You sound like Aunt Joan,' she laughed.

'That's because we think alike. It may sound exciting but be careful. Families would have been affected by these crimes. Even if it was over 80 years ago. You said there may have been two robbers that fled England. If word gets out, you don't know what people might do to keep family secrets.'

'Don't worry, we'll be careful.'

'Alright. Take care and do try to enjoy yourself, it's about time you had some fun.'

'I will. I promise, love you.'

'Love you, sweetheart.'

Jubilee booked two plane tickets to London, Heathrow. She knew this exercise wasn't going to make her rich, in fact the opposite. It would eat away at what was left of her savings. She hadn't contemplated keeping any of the jewellery that couldn't be identified. The thought of how her great-grandfather had obtained it made her blood run cold. Instead, she resigned herself to the fact that she would find the rightful owners, and in doing so, right a terrible wrong.

Meg sent an enquiry to the National Archives in England and agreed to pay the National Archives to instigate the searches they needed. Meg was worried they could search for days and find nothing, so they agreed to leave it to the professionals.

Once their appointment was confirmed with the National Archives, Jubilee emailed Henry Hawthorn to let him know they were coming to England to continue their research. Jubilee was surprised but anxious when he invited them to stay at his hotel. What if he wasn't as eager or kind as his words implied in his emails? Jubilee's caginess was returning, but notwithstanding that, she believed the Hawthorn family would want answers too. Although, she wasn't looking forward to telling Henry that her great-grandfather may have killed his great-uncle.

That night, Jubilee lay awake thinking about her great-grandfather. She wondered, how could someone simply disappear and reinvent themselves? Maybe, it was easier back then, but not today. You couldn't go to a cash machine today without the authorities knowing where, when and how much you withdrew.

At least they had identified one robbery in the Cotswolds near Cheltenham. Jubilee wondered if all the jewellery belonged to the same family or if he'd committed multiple robberies. Was Jack Jones a professional thief? How would he have known whom to burgle and where in the house he would find the jewels? Behind a painting, in a safe, in which room? Was it an inside job? Did he spend months surveying his targets? Jubilee had a restless night. Her dreams flickered from gems to break-ins to murder.

Chapter Nine

London, England
Two Weeks Later

July 5 – Wednesday afternoon – Day 1

'Now you're talking – a warm and sunny day,' Meg said, as she took off her windbreaker and tied it around her waist, as they exited Heathrow terminal.

'Let's hope it stays that way,' replied Jubilee, copying her cousin, folding her jacket up and draping it over the top of her suitcase. She thought of the scarf she had packed. Jubilee's intention was to hand it back to Henry Hawthorn, along with Jack's passport and family photo. Now, Jubilee was reluctant to part with it, as it held sentimental value and history.

Jubilee didn't want to admit it to Meg, but she was getting butterflies.

After leaving the airport, they collected their campervan. It had all the mod cons they needed, including a booklet listing all campervan and camping sites around England. Their first port of call was a supermarket where they stocked up on supplies. The second was to the nearest campervan site as jetlag was going to hit them soon. They unpacked and checked their emails for any new correspondence. Tomorrow would be the start of their adventure.

Meg had one new email.

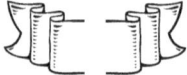

Dear Meg,

I hope you arrived safely.

I ran the background check on Jack Jones but he had no criminal record. Nothing appears in any searches until 1940 when he purchased the land your cousin currently owns. I put in a request to Scotland Yard to check if he existed in England. As it is an historic search, it may take some time. It isn't unheard of to take the name from a grave site, usually from a male child. So don't get your hopes up.

I have also searched our records for any unsolved murders in NSW in 1939 but again nothing stood out that could be related to your great-grandfather. At that time, there were no robberies in Australia relating to the calibre of jewels you claimed had been stolen. I'd say they were stolen in England and brought to Australia. Do you want me to contact Scotland Yard to investigate Jack Hawthorn's murder?

I hope you find what you're looking for.

Take care.

Your friend,
Billy

Meg replied they were going to visit the National Archives on Friday and she'd keep in touch if they had no luck.

Privately, Meg was pleased Billy was on board to assist them. She felt reassured knowing someone was watching their backs. Despite reminiscing about the annoying young boy who had slapped a paintbrush over her school dress in class.

*   *   *

July 6 – Thursday morning – Day 2

Their first stop of the day was Hatton Garden. Jubilee drove whilst Meg texted her mother instructions regarding her beloved bookshop. The bookshop opened five years ago, and Meg had never allowed herself more than a week off at any one time. Before that, Meg had been a librarian, which hadn't surprised her parents. Having an endless supply of books at her fingertips was Meg's perfect job. However, she gradually grew more restless with each passing year, until she decided to open her own bookshop. After finishing a business management degree, and with a little help from her parents, she had enough money to open The Ink in the Quill at Bowral. It was as antique as it was modern. She bought rare books from deceased estates and shelved readers' popular fiction. Book clubs would meet once a month to discuss their latest offering, while story-telling groups, enjoyed by toddlers, would sit on cushions and listen to ancient fairy tales. Meg lived in a little apartment above the shop, but below was her palace of dreams.

Jubilee had emailed Albert Bach and asked if they could visit him on Thursday. His swift response was, 'Yes. Sharp at 11:00 am.'

Blackman and Chambers had emailed to say they were unable to help with their investigation. Starr and Everett Jewellers never replied, so Jubilee and Meg decided to pay them an unexpected visit after speaking with Albert Bach.

Jubilee took the long route to Hatton Garden and drove through the heart of London. Hoping they would be forced to stop at every traffic light and pedestrian crossing they came to, they intended to take in the sights as much as possible. As they only had two weeks, they weren't sure if they'd be able to explore all the landmarks of London.

On their arrival at Hatton Garden, they were lucky to find street parking on Greville Street.

'Before we do anything, I'm having a cuppa,' Meg announced. They had an hour to kill before they met with Albert Bach so they discussed how much they should tell him. Meg put the kettle on and made them both a cup of tea. She opened a packet of biscuits to tide them over before lunch. Meg wanted to have twenty winks, but Jubilee warned her against it, otherwise she wouldn't sleep that night.

Just before 11:00 am, they walked into Lieberman and Bach. Jubilee and Meg were greeted by a very tall and immaculately dressed woman in her early sixties. She introduced herself as Tessa, Albert Bach's wife. She welcomed Jubilee and Meg and escorted them into her husband's office.

Albert Bach stood when they entered his office.

'Ah! You must be Ms Jones,' he said, shaking Jubilee's hand.

'Hello, please call me Jubilee.'

'What a lovely name.'

'Thank you, Mr Bach. May I introduce my cousin, Meg Forrester?'

'Pleasure is all mine.' Once the handshaking was over, Albert offered them a seat across from him while his wife left to make them coffee.

Albert Bach's office was chic and modern. He had a glass desk with the latest Apple computer sitting on the left side. Two family photos decorated the right side. Prints of jewellery adorned the walls, which Jubilee surmised had been designed by his family over the decades.

'Did you bring the jewellery pieces with you, Ms Jones?'

'No. I didn't think I could get them through customs without drawing suspicion. Wouldn't want to be arrested for theft,' she joked.

Albert Bach didn't find that funny.

'I have taken photos of all the jewellery I found and I will have them authenticated soon.'

'I see,' Albert Bach said, openly disappointed. 'Wise decision.'

'We were hoping you could tell us more about the pearl earrings, and the emerald set we emailed you about. More importantly who purchased them,' Meg said. 'We want to trace the original owners and learn what we can about the robbery. We've got an appointment at the National Archives in Kew tomorrow. Hopefully, they'll be able to uncover any robberies committed in 1939.'

Jubilee opened up her folder and took out the photos of the pearl earrings and a matching emerald necklace, ring, and bracelet set she had emailed to Albert recently. The dazzling necklace was inlaid with white gold. Its design was an upside-down pyramid, with four rows of emeralds. Diamonds separated the green gems in the top three rows.

'Since our last email, I've done a little digging myself.' Albert removed a folder from his in-tray and placed it on his desk. 'The original purchase was accompanied by a matching set of emerald earrings. Did you find these with the necklace?'

Albert showed Jubilee and Meg an old sketch of the earrings. It appeared to be the artist's original drawings.

'No. I'm sorry. They weren't with the jewellery I found. I can only assume they were sold long ago,' Jubilee said, feeling strangely embarrassed.

'Or they were never stolen,' Meg interjected.

'I spoke with a friend of mine whose family have been in Hatton Garden for nearly 200 years. I asked him if he knew anything about jewel robberies in the 1930s and he came back with this.' Albert handed over a copy of a newspaper article.

'What does it say, Jubes?' Meg asked.

'Police are searching for two, possibly, three men in association with the break-in at Sandalwood Lodge, near Bristol on April 22, 1939. The thieves broke into a safe and stole a large number of family heirlooms and cash.'

Jubilee looked at Albert. 'So, we have one theft near Cheltenham and one near Bristol?'

'Correct, my dear. You see, any type of jewel robbery, especially in the calibre and value that you have found, would spread around our community within days. Every jeweller would be on the lookout for someone wanting to sell them. I've asked my assistant to search our archived records for any police reports relating to robberies in 1939.'

'So, you're saying, the jewellery would have to be sold soon after they were stolen, before the police got involved,' Meg asked.

'No, not necessarily. But selling these types of jewellery would not be easy, but not impossible, unless the jeweller was unscrupulous. They would break down the pieces, as the design would be recognisable, then rebuild them into other designs, or sell the stones as individual pieces.'

'I don't suppose you know of any jeweller who would have done that?' Meg asked, cheekily.

'I'm afraid not, Ms Forrester.' Albert didn't return Meg's mischievous smile.

Jubilee continued, 'We'll add this theft at Sandalwood Lodge to our list and see if Scotland Yard has any historic records of it. Could I have the name and address of the customer who commissioned the jewellery at Bourton-on-the-Water? I believe you said in your email they purchased both the South Sea pearl earrings and the emerald necklace set.'

'I don't see why not. Although the family may not live there anymore,' Albert replied.

'Well if they did, they'd be extremely old,' Meg chuckled.

'I mean, Ms Forrester, these old houses are usually passed down through generations. Unless of course, they had to sell up because of financial difficulties. This happened quite a lot after both World Wars.'

Meg could see Albert didn't have a sense of humour. She decided to play it straight.

Jubilee knew what Albert was referring to, she remembered watching a documentary years ago about the cost of running the old castles and estates in England. Many didn't survive in the new era and were sold, while others were turned into hotels.

Albert handed Meg a photocopy of his customer's purchase receipts and their address details. Once they'd finished their coffees, they thanked him again. As they stood to leave, Meg had one final question for him.

'How much is this emerald necklace, bracelet, and ring set worth today? The back of the necklace says FL and AAA.'

'You're correct.' Albert removed another piece of paper from his folder.

'Emeralds are graded by four factors. Their colour, clarity, cut and carat weight. The highest rating is Natural AAA. Reviewing the paperwork I have in front of me, the emeralds used in the necklace were, in fact, triple A. The diamonds used were flawless. But I would need to see the necklace to authenticate it.'

'Of course, but going by your records and your company's workmanship, what is its estimated current value?' Meg repeated.

'I would estimate the necklace's value at around £500,000 and, possibly, up to a million at auction, young lady.'

'Holy fuck,' Meg said. Then, quickly adding, 'Apologies.'

'The pearl earrings could fetch up to £50,000, possibly more. As you know, once they are authenticated, the descendants of the original owners will have a case for claiming them.'

'Of course,' Jubilee said. 'I was going to hand the jewellery to the police before returning them to their new owners. They'll confirm ownership.'

'Why haven't you done this yet?'

Jubilee thought for a moment but could see no reason not to answer Albert Bach's question. 'The police investigation will be professional and pragmatic and will identify the rightful owners, but I need to know who committed those robberies and why. Was our great-grandfather involved and if so, what part did he play?'

'That's admirable of you, young lady. Well, I wish you both the best of luck.' On that note, Albert stood up, indicating the meeting was over, and showed Jubilee and Meg to the door.

Outside on the street, Jubilee said, 'Let's get back to the campervan. I want to check the map and see if Cheltenham is anywhere near Bristol.'

'My thoughts exactly. Like highwaymen.'

'Yes, but that newspaper article said two or three suspects.'

'If that report was to be believed, Jack – we'll keep calling him Jack until we figure out his real name – had an accomplice or two. One of them could be the second man they discovered in the sewer. Maybe the third thief fled to Australia with Jack.'

Jubilee pondered that idea, but everything was speculation until proven.

'If Jack had accomplices, I'm sure they would have gotten an equal share,' Jubilee stated, 'so there must be a lot more stolen than we realised. If Jack had eighteen pieces, maybe his accomplices had eighteen pieces each.'

Meg was left to ponder the same thing. Did she really want to trace them, and their families? She remembered her mother's saying about 'old wounds'.

*   *   *

Jubilee made Meg and herself a late lunch before they headed to Starr and Everett. Meg often wished she had a morsel of her cousin's culinary skills. She made cooking look easy and a joy. Meg, however, was content with doing the washing up.

Jubilee remained quiet while she ate. A new theory was niggling at her. How many men had Jack Jones killed before buying the land in Bowral? She doubted if there really was such a thing as, *honour amongst thieves*. She now realised her home was obviously bought on ill-gotten gains. This thought troubled her.

Starr and Everett was on the corner of Hatton Garden Road and St Cross Street. Upon entering the shop, they asked to speak with the owners. They gave their names but had to wait a further ten minutes before they were shown into the office of Alexandria Everett.

Jubilee and Meg introduced themselves and explained why they were there. Alexandria apologised for not responding to their email. Meg thought she appeared a little cagey and overly polite by their intrusion. Alexandria was a short woman, around fifty years old, and stood no more than five foot three inches in height. She had shiny black hair that was pulled back in a hairclip. She had an elegance about her that was accentuated by the delicate jewellery she wore.

'Please call me Alex. I'm sorry our office manager hadn't forwarded your email. We've been quite busy recently and it was probably on her to-do list.'

'It's okay, I have one of those,' Meg said, 'A to-do list that is, not an office manager.'

Alex's office was in direct contrast to the modern deco style of Albert Bach's. The walls were adorned with dark wood panelling, featuring fluted pilasters and moulded bases. It gave the appearance of stepping into the Elizabethan era. A large bookcase contained an array of non-fiction books, notably all relating to jewellery. Alex's oak desk looked to be at least 200 years old and there was a rich carpet underfoot.

Jubilee didn't want to rest on formality, so she dived straight in. 'We're hoping you could check your historical records and see who purchased this diamond necklace and a matching set of earrings.' Jubilee handed Alex the photos of the striking diamond clustered necklace in white gold, with matching earrings.

Alex looked at the notations on the back of the photo and said their records were archived and private. She apologised for not being able to help them.

Not wanting to leave empty-handed, Jubilee decided to up the ante and show her the photos of the Ruby set.

'We're also trying to identify the owner of this ruby necklace.' Jubilee removed a photo from her folder and handed it to Alex.

Meg thought she saw a flicker of recognition on Alex's face, but it was quickly replaced by a blank expression. Meg witnessed it, all the same.

'From the markings on the back, the ruby necklace was made by your family in 1939, and this diamond necklace and earrings were made well over 150 years ago, in 1866. We need to know who you made them for. I know purchase records are private but it can't hurt now, not after all this time. We believe they were stolen and we're trying to trace the rightful owners.'

'Why are you interested in stolen jewellery?' Alex asked, her eyes flared wider at Jubilee.

'Because I dug them up in my garden,' Jubilee replied.

This time, both Meg and Jubilee observed Alex's altered expression. She looked back down at the pictures for some time without saying a word. Eventually, she confirmed the markings on the jewellery were, in fact, the Starr and Everett trademark.

'If it helps your search, we believe they were stolen between March and April 1939,' Meg said.

Alex didn't need to hear anymore she pressed the intercom on her desk phone.

'Rose, can you please bring in the files for 1866 and for 1939. You'll find them in the basement against the back wall.'

After a slight pause, 'Sure thing, Alex.'

Alex's demeanour changed when she asked, 'Have you had them authenticated?'

'Not yet, I will when I return home,' Jubilee said.

'So you didn't bring them with you?'

This was the second time today that Jubilee was asked the same question.

'No.'

'Good call. Do you know anything of their history?'

'No. That's why we came to you,' Meg replied.

While they waited for Rose to return with the files, Jubilee explained to Alex how she found them and what she intended to do. When Rose entered the room, she wheeled in two old boxes on a trolley and placed them on Alex's desk. Deliberately, Rose brushed off the dust from her cashmere sweater. She announced that these old records should have been scanned into their system by now. She left Alex's office without another word.

'That was my sister, Rose,' Alex said. 'She forgets that it was her suggestion to scan and archive our old files in the first place.' Alex used a tissue to wipe the dust from the lids before opening the first one, dated 1939.

'These are our old designs and purchase records for 1939. Your ruby necklace set should be here. If they were stolen, there may be a police report here also.' Carefully, Alex searched through the documents until she found the one she was looking for.

'Here it is!' Alex put the archive box onto the floor as she placed the delicate documents on her desk.

Both Jubilee and Meg shuffled their chairs a little closer to her desk for a better look.

'The ruby set was commissioned for Sir Rupert Henley-Smith, for his wife. They lived near Bridgewater, Somerset. I believe the Henley-Smith family still live there.'

Alex also found a circular from Scotland Yard dated May 5, 1939 pertaining to the robbery. It warned of a spate of robberies that could have been linked during the previous month.

'The circular from Scotland Yard would have been sent to all jewellers in the country in case someone tried to sell them on. And these images,' Alex turned two sheets of paper around so Jubilee and Meg could see them, 'are the original designs for the ruby pieces.'

'Could we have copies of these, please? The Australian Police asked us to document everything we find,' Meg asked.

Alex studied the documents while contemplating her next move. Eventually, she agreed, gathered up all the paperwork and left her office to make photocopies for Jubilee and Meg. On her return, she handed the copies to Meg before sitting back down.

'This is great, thank you for all your help,' Meg said.

'And to think they've been sitting in a biscuit tin in your garden for over 80 years.'

Alex's demeanour had shifted again on her return to her office. She was polite enough, but Meg was sure she was still holding something back.

Alex then searched the folder marked 1866. After a few minutes she found the purchase receipts for the diamond necklace and matching earrings.

'These were made for Mr Lawrence Hardwick, at Amberley Hall, in Siddington, Cirencester.' Alex showed Jubilee and Meg the drawings of the jewellery pieces before leaving her office once again to make copies of the paperwork. On her return, she handed the copies to Meg.

'Can you give me an estimate on these jewellery sets?' Jubilee asked. 'I know you'd prefer to see the pieces in person. Considering they were made by your family, I was hoping you'd have an idea of their current value?'

'If I had to guess, going by the quality of the stones that would have been used, I would estimate the ruby set to be well over two million pounds.'

Jubilee and Meg stared at Alex with their mouths wide open. Jubilee was glad she hadn't brought the jewellery with her. Alex estimated the diamond necklace and earrings could fetch approximately £180,000 to £200,000.

Jubilee was under no illusion now of the value of her discovery.

They thanked Alex for her assistance and left.

Outside the shop, Meg couldn't wait to say, 'Well, well, well! Jack Jones was a busy boy. We have four confirmed robberies.'

'Don't joke, Meg. He was obviously a career criminal.' Jubilee looked up and down the street, calculating her next move. 'I don't want to visit these estates without having all the facts first. Let's wait until we've visited the National Archives tomorrow and see what they've uncovered for us.'

'Agreed. We can record what we've found out so far. I think jetlag has just kicked in again.' Meg's eyes started to droop, uncontrollably.

'You're not half wrong. I feel twenty years older in a day,' yawned Jubilee.

Jubilee and Meg headed to a campervan site closest to Kew in Richmond, Surrey. They decided to take a long walk around the picturesque town before jetlag forced them to retire for the night.

*   *   *

'Take a look at this!' Alex Everett showed her sister Rose a photocopy of the ruby necklace Jubilee had found. 'Ms Jones confirmed she has the entire set – if she's to be believed.'

'Well, if she has the set, it belongs to us, not the bloody Henley-Smiths.'

'Our grandfather will finally be vindicated,' Alex said, shaking her head in amazement.

'Did they bring the ruby set with them?'

'No.'

'What are we going to do about it?'

'Get it back, of course.'

Rose looked solemnly at her sister. 'The authorities had insinuated the robbery was an inside job. Pointing their bigoted fingers at us. It was easier to blame the Jew than the Lord of the Manor. It nearly broke Grandfather when they accused him of being involved. If these two women start poking around in the past, we may actually find out the truth. 'The Flame of India' nearly brought this firm to its knees. If Ms Jones is truly going to hand that jewellery back, we need to be there when she does.'

Alex nodded at her sister. 'Call Lockwood. I want to know our legal rights.'

'Will do,' Rose said, walking back into her own office.

Alex sat in her office staring down at the picture of the Flame of India. She grew angrier by the minute. It had been so easy for her grandfather's contemporaries to insinuate his involvement in the robberies, and in doing so, deflect their own. *Jealously breeds contempt*, she thought. *The Henley-Smiths were going to pay for their lies.*

The only certainty Alex knew was that their grandfather died a broken man, his name forever smeared by lies. She would see to it that his reputation would be avenged – at any cost.

Chapter Ten

National Archive, Kew, Richmond

July 7 – Friday morning – Day 3

'*Please*,' Meg humbly implored Jubilee, 'when in Rome.'

Jubilee relented and made them a full English breakfast before driving to the National Archives in Kew. Their appointment was at 10:00 am. They had already booked a viewing room and were anxious to learn what the researcher had unearthed. On their arrival, they provided their reader's ticket and were shown into the reading room. The researcher arrived shortly after and introduced herself as Helena.

When they all made themselves comfortable, Helena began.

'Your search criteria was in relation to the death of Jack Hawthorn in Plymouth 1939 and any information pertaining to robberies along the west coast, specifically targeting large estates in 1939.'

'Yes, that's correct,' Jubilee confirmed, unable to hide her excitement. 'Please tell me you found something.'

'Well, I'm pleased to say I have found a number of articles relating to Jack Hawthorn.' Helena placed two folders on the table, one of which was considerably thicker than the other and opened the first one labelled 'Jack Hawthorn'. Both girls shuffled up as close as they could to the table, forgetting the across-table politeness and relaxed COVID restrictions.

'He was the second son of Robert and Eleanor Hawthorn. Born May 6, 1915. Died 1939. He was educated at Oxford with a degree in business and commerce. He was scheduled to leave for Australia on May 2, 1939 from Plymouth on board the *Jervis Bay*, a large passenger cargo ship. However, his body was found in a sewer in July 1940. He was identified by a label sewn onto his clothing and a family ring still in his possession.' Helena placed a police report, including photos, in front of Jubilee and Meg. The police photos were pretty grim.

'I also found a few letters written to Scotland Yard, by Eleanor Hawthorn, enquiring after her missing son. There was also a note in the police report compiled by Scotland Yard from the harbour master in Sydney, Australia, confirming his arrival on the *Jervis Bay*. So, I'm assuming someone stole his identity.'

'Yes,' Jubilee interrupted. 'I was told the same thing by a relative of Eleanor Hawthorn.'

Helena continued, 'Eleanor Hawthorn hired a private investigator at Carlson & Son to find her son and offered a reward for any information relating to her son's disappearance. The private investigator had put out flyers around Plymouth, but I couldn't find anything relating to her success in that matter. The private investigator firm no longer exists and as you know, the war broke out and everything changed, sharpish. However, the police had no suspects for his murder. To this day, the second victim in the sewer has not been identified.'

Helena handed Jubilee and Meg more paperwork. They remained silent, but very intrigued.

'The last document I have is a newspaper clipping on the notification of Jack Hawthorn's burial in St Ives, Cornwall.'

Helena handed over the final document and the folder to Jubilee to keep. Jubilee was a little disappointed, given she was hoping to learn more about the real Jack Hawthorn. Jubilee's only other avenue now rested with Henry Hawthorn. She hoped he could shed more light on his family background.

'Regarding the robberies I had considerably more luck.' Helena opened the second folder, which contained a report compiled by Scotland Yard on each of the five robberies. Witness statements, forensic reports, including fingerprint analyses, newspaper articles and death certificates. Helena went on to say that Scotland Yard believed all five robberies were committed by the same perpetrators. On a separate piece of paper was a full description of all the jewellery pieces stolen from each estate.

'Jackpot!' Jubilee said.

Finally, Jubilee and Meg had the full description of what had been stolen. They recognised some descriptions of the stolen jewellery straight away, although the list had quite a lot more pieces on it than Jubilee had in her biscuit tin.

Helena then read a police report on the death of a man named Tom Fields, found shot to death on the outskirts of Bridgewater on April 30, 1939.

'He was a known thief and upon providing his photo to the family at Grimshaw Manor in Bath, he was identified as one of the robbers.'

Jubilee and Meg were mesmerised as more and more history unfolded.

'The police stated he was known to have travelled in the company of a Hughie McBean. However, the police had no evidence linking this man as his accomplice on these robberies. Although, they believed it highly likely that he was the second perpetrator. The police also surmised there must have been a falling out and the two men fought on the road to Bridgewater. They searched for Hughie McBean but found no trace of him. However, there may have been a third accomplice, because during the final robbery at Harrowgate Hall, a witness stated she saw two men escaping down the servant's stairwell, who then ran through the kitchen. The kitchenhand said she heard one man yell to the other, "Hurry up, Mallard".'

'That's amazing,' Meg said.

Helena handed the photocopies of the witness statements to her.

'I ran a trace on the name Mallard but nothing came up in the police reports. You may need to search for him elsewhere, if you feel he's important to your research.'

Jubilee and Meg were impressed.

'Mallard may be a relative of Tom Fields or Hughie McBean?' Jubilee offered up. She wondered if they would have any luck tracing him on Ancestry.

'It's all here in Scotland Yard's report.' Helena handed over the folder. Jubilee was so excited she jumped up and hugged Helena, then quickly composed herself.

'I'm glad we could be of help to you,' Helena replied, a little taken aback.

'You have no idea,' Meg said with a laugh.

'Thank you, so much,' Jubilee said again. Jubilee and Meg gathered up the two folders and left the National Archives enthusiastically. They finally felt like they were getting somewhere.

Back in the campervan, Jubilee said, 'Okay, if this Hughie McBean was one of the thieves, then we only have to identify the third man, Mallard.'

'That might be tricky,' Meg said. 'We only have his first name or surname to go by.'

'At least we know which robberies took place in which order, and we can match the jewellery to their owners. Do you think McBean or Mallard killed Tom Fields? Maybe they didn't want to split everything three ways.'

'Possibly,' Meg said. 'Or, maybe, he attacked them?'

'If Tom Fields was found dead, maybe Mallard stole the identity of the second victim found in the sewer and both men left on the *Jervis Bay*. It's good we now have two names which could be our great-grandfather, Hughie McBean, or Mallard.'

'Great! What a choice we have. A blaggard or a blaggard.'

'We've got a lot to get through. Let's head down to Plymouth, I want to see where Jack Hawthorn's body was found. We can find a campsite there and spend the rest of the day going over what we've discovered. I need to catalogue all this information.'

'Okay,' Meg said. 'Now that we have identified the owners, we can start to trace their ancestors. If the families still reside in those houses, it will be easy enough to contact them. I'll also create more searches on Ancestry.'

'That sounds like a plan,' Jubilee said.

'Billy will confirm who will legally inherit. I'll send him another email to start investigating these families. They'll need to provide a will detailing the ownership. If there is no will, I presume the jewels will go to the closest blood relative. Who knows, it may be different in England. These old houses were passed down from father to son, while the wife and daughters got allowances and so on. You saw what happened to the Dashwoods in Sense and Sensibility. They were out on their ears with a pittance.'

Jubilee laughed at her cousin. A true feminist, yet she had a point. 'Since when have you been calling him Billy, and not Sergeant Baker?'

'Since he asked me to.'

Jubilee smiled at her cousin and said no more on the subject.

Meg drove the campervan out of Kew and onto the M3, then onto the A303. They arrived in Plymouth after 3:00 pm. The Riverside Caravan Park was just off the A38.

Both women had been so engrossed by their discovery and what should be their next move that they barely noticed the beautiful scenery on their journey. On arrival, they ate a late lunch and took themselves off for a long walk to stretch their legs through the Dartmoor National Park, before photographing and documenting all the information Helena had provided.

Back at the campervan, Jubilee marked the locations of the five robberies in the order in which they were committed on her map. They began on April 16, 1939 and ended on April 28. Then, she matched each piece of jewellery in her biscuit tin to the estate they were stolen from.

Strangely, she didn't have any items stolen from Grimshaw Manor, despite the police report stating eight pieces of jewellery had been stolen. Jubilee asked Meg if they should bother that family, considering they had nothing to present to them. Meg convinced Jubilee to visit the estate, as they might have further insight into the robbery that Helena couldn't provide.

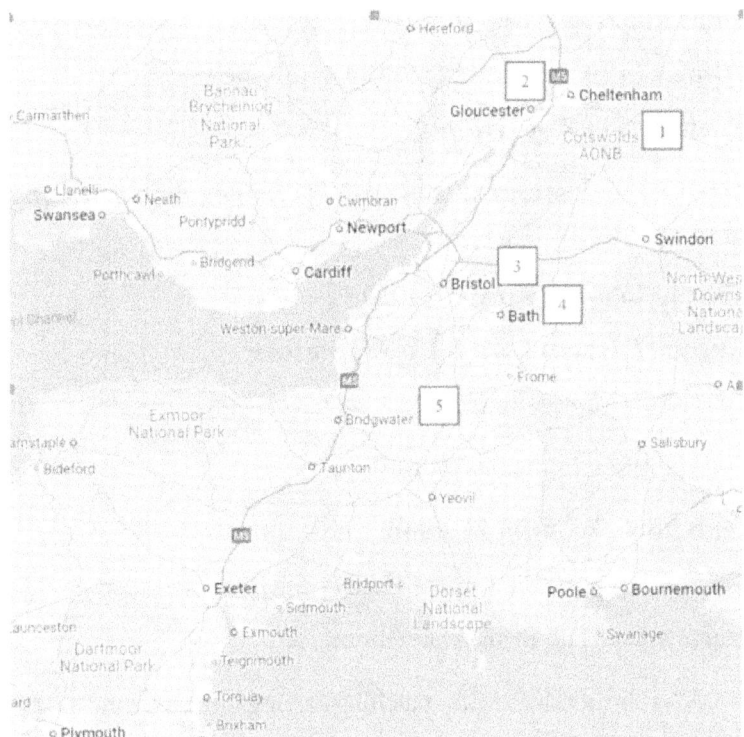

First Robbery: April 16, 1939

Current Owners: James & Clarissa Hawkins

Bromley House, Bourton-on-the-Water, Cotswold, Cheltenham.

> One pair of earrings, South Sea pearls with diamonds inlaid in white gold. One emerald necklace, with matching ring and bracelet (earrings missing).

Second Robbery: April 19, 1939

Current Owners: Jonathan & Emma Hardwick

Amberley Hall, Siddington, Cirencester, Gloucestershire.

> One necklace, a tiara, one pair of earrings, and a brooch.

Third Robbery: April 22, 1939

Owners in 1939: Harold & Emily Brunswick

Sandalwood Lodge, Bristol.

> One necklace, a matching pair of earrings, three rings, and a pendant.

Fourth Robbery: April 26, 1939

Current Owners: Lord & Lady Grimshaw

Grimshaw Manor, Bath.

> Nothing in the biscuit tin

Fifth Robbery: April 28, 1939

Current owners: Sir Rupert Henley-Smith

Harrowgate Hall, Bridgewater, Somerset.

> A ruby necklace, with matching earrings, bracelet, and a ring.

*   *   *

After the list was compiled, Jubilee sighed. 'There's a lot missing, Meg. I suppose Jack's accomplices took their share, or he sold some to purchase the land in Bowral.'

'We had to expect that. At least we've matched what you found.'

'Do you think we'll ever find the remainder of the jewellery?'

Meg sighed. 'No. I don't think so, Jubes. Remember what Albert Bach said, that the jewellery could have been broken down and sold as individual pieces long ago. Let's just focus on what we have and let sleeping dogs lie.'

'You're right.'

*   *   *

That evening, Jubilee sat outside the campervan enjoying a glass of red wine. Now that she had a list of all the estates robbed in April 1939, she hoped to uncover the extent of her great-grandfather's crimes. Yet, she also felt very nostalgic, knowing she was about to rewrite history in a country steeped in centuries of history. Where every cobblestone street could tell a tale of past misdeeds. A country that recorded every battle, every tragedy, every triumph, and every bloody royal command in its history books. With anticipation, Jubilee realised she was about to accomplish something extraordinary, and in doing so, record her own small portion of history.

That night, Jubilee fell into a deep sleep, and never once dreamt about her own unwritten future back home.

Chapter Eleven

A Private Gentlemen's Club, London

July 7 – Friday evening

'Are you sure?' Giles snapped.

'Of course I'm bloody sure and keep your voice down. It's all over town. Someone has finally found those bloody jewels,' Louis snapped.

'All of them?'

'Unknown, but my source said they visited Starr and Everett.'

'Fuck! Did they bring the jewellery with them?'

'I doubt it.'

'You need to make sure and find out whatever else they've uncovered.'

'I'm on it.'

'This could end badly for both of us.'

'No kidding. Just hold your nerve. What about your friend, Rupert?'

'I'll talk to him. He's more scared of scandal than we are.'

Chapter Twelve

Plymouth

July 8 – Saturday morning – Day 4

'Crap, it's cold!' shivered Meg, as she stepped outside and breathed in the chilly morning air. 'It's supposed to be summer.' Her usually chic shoulder-length hair was uncharacteristically electrified all around her head as it hadn't had its morning comb. She quickly stepped back inside the campervan and put the kettle on. She squeezed into the little toilet cubicle and then splashed some cold water on her face to wake up.

She gave Jubilee a coffee and some burnt toast before she hopped on the computer to see if they had any more emails and contact traces on Ancestry. She had created two searches, Tom (Thomas) Fields and Hughie (Hugh) McBean. Meg didn't have enough on Mallard to warrant an accurate search.

Meg found three new emails. One was from the Plymouth Library confirming they could assist in their research. The second was from a fourth jeweller confirming the two pieces they emailed were indeed made by their company. One tiara and a necklace. Their details matched the police report Helena had given them. Meg was satisfied with how everything was coming together. The third email was from Billy back home in Bowral. He confirmed the receipt of the documents she had sent him and that he had started the investigation into the families of the victims in 1939. He also wrote that he would instigate an investigation with Scotland Yard into Tom Fields and Hughie McBean. Meg smiled at his professionalism. He also provided her with his personal mobile if she needed to contact him urgently. He ended the email by asking Meg to be careful. His words made her blush, in a way she hadn't in a long time.

After Jubilee brushed her teeth again, to remove the burnt charcoal bits between her teeth, they drove to Plymouth. As she drove, she could feel herself growing tense again. She was eager for answers, but at the same time, she was afraid of what she would discover. Did their great-grandfather kill Tom Fields? Did he also kill Jack Hawthorn simply to steal his identity? It wasn't only her great-grandfather that frustrated her. She was free from work, free from debt, free from commitments, free to travel and explore. However, she didn't truly feel free. What was next for her once her adventure was over? Was she supposed to return home and start again in another restaurant back in Sydney or Bowral? Would that never-ending feeling of being one step behind everyone else re-surface? She didn't want to return to that. Her one night's break from her maudlin thoughts had evaporated in the light of a new day. Jubilee turned the radio on for distraction.

Upon arrival in Plymouth, Jubilee and Meg headed for the library. As they walked through the ancient naval town, Jubilee told Meg that once they'd visited Plymouth library, she wanted to go to Cheltenham and visit the first estate on the list. Afterwards, they would be able to travel down the coast, stopping off at the other four estates. If the families no longer lived there, they would obtain Sergeant Banker's assistance to trace them. Jubilee was conscious about how much time they had left in England.

'Sounds like a plan, Jubes,' Meg replied. 'Except what if we can't trace the descendants, will you apply to keep those pieces?'

'I don't know. If the police have no luck, do you think I should?'

'Yes, I do. They need to belong to someone. You haven't done anything wrong and we're doing everything we can to identify and trace the owners. Their sale could allow you to own your own restaurant.'

'That's what my mum said. I'm not sure if I want to, though. Besides, I don't want to get my hopes up. I started this journey to solve a mystery.'

'And we will.'

'Also, I thought, what if the owners start their own investigations into the other two men in a bid to get the rest of their jewellery back? What if they locate Hughie McBean and Mallard's descendants? Is it possible to sue all of us for what was stolen? What if they find out Jack Jones sold their jewellery to buy the land in Bowral? What if they want compensation?'

'Calm down, Jubes, you're jumping ahead of yourself,' Meg said, waving her hands downwards in front of her. 'We may be their descendants.' But her cousin had a good point. Meg hadn't thought about that. For the first time since starting their journey, Meg feared that Jubilee's expectations would not play out as she hoped. She made a mental note to email Billy and ask him about the laws surrounding the purchase of property with stolen goods.

'We can only return the jewellery you've found. No one can prove where the money came from to buy the acres in Bowral.'

Both women walked quietly to the library as they each thought of the consequences that could arise from their undertaking.

Chapter Thirteen

Plymouth Library

July 8 – Saturday mid-morning – Day 4

Jubilee and Meg arrived at the Plymouth library a little after 10:00 am. Meg knew how to search through the old newspaper records from her days as a librarian.

They started their search one month before the *Jervis Bay* left port for Australia. They searched for anything related to or concerning the murder of Jack Hawthorn.

They found articles in the local papers about the robberies. As Helena had already provided copies of them, they continued their search for anything new.

Meg found another article on the death of Tom Fields and read it to Jubilee.

'*A man identified as Tom Fields was found dead along a roadside north of Bridgewater. He had been shot. The motive for the killing is unknown, but his personal possessions were missing. He was identified by his fingerprints which were already on file with Scotland Yard. He was known to the police and had spent time in jail for previous robbery offences. The police believe he may have been involved in a spate of robberies along the west coast.*'

Meg read out another article. '*The police are searching for two more men involved in a spate of robberies. A known accomplice of Tom Fields is still on the loose. A third man is still unidentified.*'

'There had to have been a fight between two or three of them,' Jubilee said.

'Possibly, but if Hughie was a known accomplice of Tom, wouldn't that imply they were friends? You know the term, "as thick as thieves". Wouldn't that make them close?'

'True, but maybe the other guy, Mallard, killed Tom, and Hughie fled?'

Months on, they found advertisements in the local newspapers offering a reward for information pertaining to a missing person, Jack Hawthorn. There was a picture of him with contact details for private investigators, Carlson & Son. It wasn't until the following year that a series of articles appeared announcing the death of Jack Hawthorn. Meg found a follow-up of articles in the local papers regarding the discovery of two bodies found in a sewer. A week later, another advertisement appeared offering a reward for information regarding Jack Hawthorn's death.

'Poor woman,' Jubilee said. 'She must have been so desperate.'

'I wonder if she ever got any replies.'

'If she did, hopefully, Henry can find something in his family's records.'

'Let's hope so. I bet Eleanor received a lot of bogus replies, you know, people simply after the reward.'

Jubilee printed the articles they found and added them to her folder.

After leaving the library, they decided to take a walk around Plymouth. They ended their walk down at the same cobblestone lane that housed the sewer that Jack Hawthorn's decaying body was discovered in. The same manhole cover was still there. It felt surreal to Jubilee to be standing above where his body had laid all those years ago, undiscovered. Possibly, where their great-grandfather once stood and fought before disposing of Jack's body.

Jubilee shivered. The lane felt eerie, so they returned to the main road, located not far from the seafront. Jubilee scanned the street and noticed a number of old shops and pubs and wondered if they had been open on the night before the *Jervis Bay* departed in 1939. How did their great-grandfather get a strong, healthy, and intelligent young man like Jack Hawthorn into an alleyway and kill him? Did he get him drunk at one of the local pubs first and then lure him outside to his death?

Jubilee wanted to leave Plymouth. She was eager to head north and visit the first estate robbed in April 1939 – Bromley House, near Bourton-on-the-Water. It was still owned by the Hawkins family.

They drove on the M5 past Bridgewater, then past Bristol and up towards Gloucester. While Meg drove, Jubilee finally relaxed and took in all the breathtaking scenery. It was luscious and green, not something she could always attribute to Bowral when the rain didn't come and the hot dry weather burnt the valley yellow.

James Hawkins had replied to Jubilee's email the night before and said he would be happy to meet with them. He agreed to search through his family records and pull out anything relating to the historic robbery. Jubilee received confirmation from him that he would be available to meet at his estate at 9:00 am the next day.

*   *   *

On their arrival at Bourton-on-the-Water, Jubilee and Meg found the nearest campervan site and booked themselves in for the night. They spent the rest of the afternoon walking along the magnificent canal. As the sun shone down on the leafy trees running along the canal, Jubilee characterised the moment as 'picture postcard perfect' in all its vibrant splendour. Everything was bursting with life as the days grew longer and warmer heading deeper into summer. They were joined by many other tourists during their journey, who had the same idea.

Jubilee felt like a traitor. She loved Bowral, but at Bourton-on-the-Water there wasn't a gum or eucalyptus tree in sight. It was a different type of beauty. She was both growing to love England, while it was making her homesick. Returning to Bowral during the pandemic had made her fall in love with it all over again. Here in England, she was seeing a new beauty again in the world.

By the canal, Jubilee felt very relaxed as she strolled with Meg. Jubilee couldn't recall when she last went on holiday. Then she remembered. About ten years ago her mother, aunt and uncle and her cousins took a P&O cruise around Fiji and Samoa for two weeks. Jubilee realised how fleeting time was. She missed those fun family days.

At sixteen, she left school after being offered an apprenticeship as a trainee in a Bowral restaurant. Then she enrolled in TAFE. As expected in her field as a professional chef, Jubilee had worked long hours, most evenings and weekends.

Meg wasn't much better. Her bookshop had kept her busy for years. Open seven days, the weekend was always her busiest trade. Although she had staff to help her, she always kept a close eye on her shop. It hadn't left her much time for socialising either. Nevertheless, Meg had a greater passion for books than people and kept herself closeted away in her shop most days.

If Jubilee opened her own restaurant, the hours would be even longer. The required capital needed would be substantial and the risk could be even greater. She was at a loss to know what to do. She hadn't worked as a professional chef for over two years, she did miss it, but not the sense of feeling out of place in her life at times.

They eventually stopped for coffee, which gave Meg the opportunity to video call her mother. As instructed by Meg's mother, they spent the rest of the afternoon sightseeing and shopping. They drifted into a lively pub where they spent the rest of the evening. Only once did Jubilee's thoughts drift back into the murky past of 1939.

*   *   *

The next morning, Jubilee stepped out of the campervan and stretched for a few minutes. Today was going to be an exciting day. They were heading to the sight of the first robbery. Jubilee thought about Bromley House and grew anxious about meeting James Hawkins. What if it all backfired? She had imagined it a hundred times, how it would go down meeting the descendants and sharing their discovery. Seeing their smiling faces at their windfall. Now that it was actually happening, she felt dread.

No regrets, she thought to herself before closing the door. *I have to stop being so bloody afraid all the time.*

Chapter Fourteen

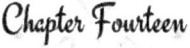

Bromley House, Cotswold, Cheltenham
Home of James and Clarissa Hawkins

July 9 – Sunday – Day 5

*M*eg drove the campervan down the long driveway where ancient oak trees stood to attention on either side for centuries. Bromley House was a 17th-century country estate. The front façade was red brick with twenty-eight windows looking out onto a neatly manicured garden. The house stood four storeys, which included four windows protruding from the attic. The lower level was partially below ground. Meg surmised it housed the kitchens, cellars and servant's quarters in centuries long forgotten.

'Wow,' was all Jubilee could muster, as she stepped out of the campervan and looked up at the enormous house.

'Yeah … but a bugger to clean,' Meg replied, as she pulled on her cardigan again, and wondered if it had a library. She knew these old country estates had libraries. Meg hoped James Hawkins would let her visit his library before they left.

James Hawkins appeared by the front door to greet his guests. As they approached, Jubilee noticed the discreet security cameras by the front door as she entered. They were the only modern devices to give away the century they were living in. They shook James's hand warmly before he invited them inside. In contrast to the façade, the foyer was chic and modern with marble floors. A round table showcased the centre of the room with one of the largest flower displays Jubilee had ever seen. Jubilee didn't feel so bad with all this wealth on display. Bromley House was grand and impressive, inside and out.

James showed them into the garden room which was located at the back of the house. It was over 60 feet in length with glass windows running along the length of the room. Even on the chilliest days, the sun's rays could burst through the windows adding brightness and warmth without the cold autumn and winter winds intruding. The garden room had two sets of seating areas, one looking out over the garden while the second was at the other end of the room facing a fireplace. There were palms and indoor plants scattered throughout the room imparting a feeling of being connected to the magnificently manicured garden, which resided on the other side of the glass windows. The whole room was enchanting, right down to the mosaic tiles that adorned the floor.

Meg could see that the garden stretched down to a tranquil lake lined with ageless trees in an abundance of colour. She was dying to pull out her mobile and film it. Her mother would be envious.

Instead, James offered them a seat as the housekeeper arrived carrying a tray of drinks and cakes.

'I have to say your email took me by surprise. I was a little dubious,' he said.

'I'm sorry, that wasn't our intention,' Jubilee replied. 'I'd like to elaborate on why we're here.'

Jubilee explained how she had found the biscuit tin buried in her back garden in Bowral, and what was inside it. She opened her folder and handed James the photos of the jewellery that originated from Bromley House. She also provided him with the police report identifying all the items stolen during the robbery. Meg asked him if he had found any records or proof of ownership regarding the jewellery that she had emailed him.

James had his own folder, which had been placed on the coffee table. He removed some old paperwork from Lieberman and Bach. The documents were purchase receipts for the golden South Sea pearls and the emerald jewellery set. The only item missing from the purchase docket was the emerald earrings. James noted there were approximately eight more pieces missing that were listed as stolen from Bromley House. Sadly, Jubilee confirmed she didn't have them in her possession.

Everyone remained silent as they each read through the documents they were given, until James finally spoke.

'I'm astounded. The only reason I agreed to meet with you was because I recognised the emerald necklace in the pictures you sent me. Would you come with me a moment?' James stood up and gestured with his hand for them to follow him.

Jubilee and Meg looked at each other and shrugged but agreed. They followed James out of the room and into a library that was bigger than Jubilee's house. Bookcases ran along two of the walls all the way up to the ceiling. There were ladders hooked up to rollers that ran along each wall to help reach the higher resting books. The walls and desk were made of a dark mahogany wood. A deep burgundy leather lounge suite sat facing another fireplace, with a thick rug underfoot for the coldest of nights. For Meg, it was the perfect setting to snuggle up in on cold nights for an evening of reading by a fire. This room was in direct contrast to the upgrades Jubilee and Meg had witnessed entering the house. It had been untouched by modern intervention, and it was obvious the Hawkins family wanted to preserve the antiquity of this room. Jubilee and Meg felt like they had just stepped back in time.

Meg was in heaven and didn't know where to look first. However, James walked over to the far wall. He wanted Jubilee and Meg to see the portrait that hung over the fireplace.

'This is what I wanted to show you. This was my great-grandmother, Theresa Hawkins.' Both Jubilee and Meg admired the portrait. Not because of the skill of the artist, as they couldn't confirm a likeness, but because of what Theresa was wearing around her neck – the emerald necklace. She was also wearing the matching earrings, bracelet and ring. The green gems sparkled brightly under the light above the portrait.

Jubilee's heart skipped a beat.

'Oh my god!'

'Holy shit!' Meg overstated.

'Then they really do belong to you, James.'

'I don't know what to say,' he replied. 'You could have kept them and said nothing.'

'I couldn't do that. Besides what would I do with them? Wear them to the local Bowral RSL club?' Jubilee chuckled. 'They don't belong to me or my family, we've had them for far too long. They need to come home.'

James escorted them back into the garden room. He went on to explain what he knew about the robbery and the aftermath of it.

'From what I discovered in my grandmother Eleanor Hawkins's diaries, the thieves broke in very early on the morning of April 16 and managed to open the safe. They stole twelve pieces of jewellery. We kept the police report of the items stolen for insurance purposes.' He handed over another document to Meg. It was similar to the documentation they obtained at the National Archives. 'As the thieves were leaving, Theresa, my great-grandmother, who was obviously a light sleeper, awoke when she heard something. She came out of her bedroom to see what the noise was and saw two men running down the stairs from the second floor. One of the men knocked her down and she suffered a head wound. She eventually recovered, but wasn't able to identify either man as it was too dark and they wore balaclavas. The police returned a few weeks later and showed them a photograph of a man who was found dead near the outskirts of Bridgewater but she wasn't able to help them. She couldn't say what they were wearing or how tall they were. I'd say she would have been in shock.'

'I'm so sorry,' Jubilee said, beginning to feel guilty.

'Could there have been three men?' Meg asked James. 'We have three possible names associated with the robberies.'

'I'm not sure. Eleanor stated in her diary that Theresa only saw two men. Are you sure your great-grandfather was one of these men?'

'Yes, we think so,' Meg said. 'We're just not sure which one he was.'

'Jack Jones is a common enough name,' James said. 'It's an easy name to blend into society with.'

'True. We think the thieves may have split the jewellery between them. There were only eighteen items in the biscuit tin. Considerably more was stolen, so we may never know what happened to the rest.'

'I understand. I'm amazed you found the emeralds and pearl earrings. My wife, Clarissa warned me to be careful of you. She thought this might be a hoax or scam. However, when I recognised the emerald necklace, I knew you were telling the truth. Clarissa's away at the moment, visiting her mother. She'll be thrilled when I present her the missing jewellery.'

'I'm glad,' said Jubilee, with some relief.

James Hawkins asked the only question not yet answered, 'Why didn't you just give the jewellery to the police to investigate?'

Jubilee looked down at her hands, she twirled her ring around and around on her finger before answering. She looked over at James and said, 'There's a story to unravel, and I have too many question marks that need resolving. We're in contact with the police back home, but for personal reasons, I needed to know what happened in 1939 and what part our great-grandfather played in it.'

'That's admirable of you. I think I would want to know also.'

'Thanks.'

'No! Thank you for returning the jewellery. I don't know what to say.'

'You don't have to say anything. When we return home, I'll confirm your proof of ownership with the police before I have them transferred back to England. If you don't have all the relevant paperwork, I'm sure the police will be able to verify your claim through other means.'

James thanked them again. This wasn't what he expected when he woke up that morning. He said he would keep looking for the remaining receipts, but considering Jubilee only had a few of his family's heirlooms it would be a fruitless venture.

Jubilee, Meg, and James talked for another hour. He took them for a walk around the grounds of the estate while Meg took a thousand photographs for her mother. The gardens were inspiring and beautiful to walk through. Great care must have gone into their design. The garden's size matched the house perfectly. Meg couldn't decide what had more grandeur, the gardens or the house.

They eventually returned to the house and shook hands before saying their final goodbyes.

Jubilee promised James she would be in contact once they returned to Bowral. She gave him her mobile number before she stepped into the campervan.

*   *   *

By 12:30 pm, Meg and Jubilee were back on the road, heading towards Siddington in Cirencester. Amberley Hall was the location of the second robbery and the second estate they planned to visit.

They hadn't received a reply to their email from Amberley Hall. They tried calling, however, the number on their website only went to voicemail. Jubilee said, 'Amberley Hall's website stated they're open to visitors on Saturdays, Sundays, Mondays, and Tuesdays. Let's find a new campsite and visit Amberley Hall tomorrow. We're in luck. It's still owned by the same family.'

'Sounds like a plan. Well! That went better than I thought it would,' Meg said.

'Yes. It did,' Jubilee replied, not sounding convinced.

'What's wrong?'

'Theresa Hawkins could have died during that robbery. I hope it wasn't Jack who hit her. Do you think he even gave a damn?'

'Look, Jubes. Whatever took place back then has nothing to do with you. Don't forget that. You're trying to right a wrong, which is commendable, but don't go blaming yourself for what he did.'

'I know. But I'm living in a house on a sizable block of land, which I've just inherited all thanks to five robberies.'

'That's right, and my mum and dad own their home thanks to her share of the inheritance. You can't undo the past. Only learn from it. And that's exactly why we're here. Learning what Jack Jones did. Or whatever the fuck his name was – McBean or Mallard.'

'You're right. I'm being maudlin.'

'Look! In the worst case scenario someone might sue you for the rest of their missing jewellery. Does that make you feel better?'

'Shit, I forgot about that. Do you think they will? Is that possible?'

'I'm not sure, to be honest,' Meg said. She paused to think. 'If Jack Jones was a thief, then he was always a thief. How many other homes had he robbed prior to 1939?'

Meg had a point, but Jubilee still couldn't help but feel responsible.

As Meg drove, Jubilee added James's papers to her own folder and recorded the date and time.

It had turned into another glorious day by the time Jubilee and Meg stopped at a quaint village pub for a late lunch. The temperature had risen to twenty-two degrees. They lingered too long in the village before Jubilee had to pry Meg out of another antique bookshop.

They recommenced their journey back on the A429 towards Siddington. This time Jubilee drove, while Meg enjoyed the countryside as it amiably passed by. Although she kept wondering how her bookshop was fairing under the care of her mother and her sister, Jodie. She sent her mother a quick text.

They drew closer to Siddington and the next estate, Amberley Hall.

Chapter Fifteen

Bowral

July 9 – Sunday night

*T*he assailant wrapped a towel around his elbow to protect himself before breaking the windowpane. He opened the window from the inside and entered the house. He knew what he was looking for, and quickly rummaged through the house, not caring about the personal value of the items he damaged during his search.

He turned over the bedroom, searching through the drawers, under mattresses and in the wardrobes. He tossed Jubilee's jumpers and blankets across the bed, but the assailant couldn't find what he was looking for. He walked through the entire house but found nothing. Swearing aloud, he pulled out his mobile and made a long-distance phone call.

'I've searched everywhere and I'm telling you nothing's here. Are you sure she doesn't have them with her?'

Ten thousand miles away, Louis swore. 'Yes, of course. Did you check the kitchen? Pull the kitchen apart. Is there a garage or garden shed?'

'Yes, and I checked there first.'

'Shit! She's probably deposited them in a bank, that's what I would have done. Are you sure there's nothing else there that looks incriminating?'

'I've found nothing.'

'Okay, it was worth a try. Come home.'

The assailant left the way he came in. Swearing under his breath, it had been a bloody long trip for nothing.

*   *   *

'Shit!' cursed Louis. He had been enjoying his Sunday golf match. He knew Miss Jones wouldn't have left the jewellery at home, but he had to make sure. Louis made another call.

'It's me!'

'Well?' snapped Giles.

'I could have told you the jewellery wouldn't be there. But I'm confident she only has a portion of it.'

'How so?'

'If she had it all, she would have asked my firm to identify more of the pieces stolen.'

'If she's a descendant of our man, she might know the whereabouts of the remaining jewellery. He wouldn't simply hide the remaining pieces without leaving a clue or note as to their whereabouts.'

'He may have stashed it here in England before he fled or hid it after arriving in Australia. It could be anywhere. Maybe it's best left buried – along with what your family did.'

'Your family is also implicated, remember that. Those women will eventually come here. I told my housekeeper to say we were overseas. It won't hold them off for long.'

'That was pointless. Find out what you can from them. If Miss Jones found the jewellery by chance, she might not know the significance of what or where she found it. Ask her!'

'I won't have my family dragged through the mud for what my grandfather did over 80 years ago. My father always said it would come back to haunt us.'

'Stop whining, Giles. They'll stop by and ask you about the stolen jewellery, you confirm what was taken, and ask your own questions. Then, they'll be on their way.'

'Where are they now?'

'They're at a caravan site in Cirencester, not far from Amberley Hall. We've been following them. I'll have someone check their campervan to see what information they've uncovered so far.'

'Fine. But if this comes back to bite my family, it's going to gnaw at yours.' On that note, the phone went dead.

Louis shoved his phone back in his pocket. He needed to calm down. This next hole was a tricky one. He had always known about the robberies in 1939. His father had told him the story many years ago. He knew how his family made their fortune, but he didn't rightly care. His hands were clean. Still, his company's reputation was at stake and that was entirely another matter.

Louis stepped back from the tee and placed another call to an associate, instructing him to stay close to Miss Jones and Miss Forrester. At the first opportunity, he was to enter the campervan and search inside.

Louis picked up his driver and walked up to the tee again. He closed his eyes and focused on the job at hand. He was already two shots behind his partner, and he wasn't a man who liked to lose.

Chapter Sixteen

Siddington, Cirencester

July 9 – Sunday

*I*t was early evening. Meg and Jubilee were about to head into town for dinner when Meg's mobile chimed. She had a text message from her mother:

Call me ASAP.

Meg opened up her laptop and video called her mother.

'Hi, darling, how's it going over there?' was her first question.

'Good Mum, we've spoken to the owner of some of the pieces in Jubilee's biscuit tin. Hopefully tomorrow, we'll speak to another.'

'That's great! Look, is Jubilee there?'

'Yes. Jubes, Mum wants a word.'

After drying her hands, Jubilee put down the tea towel and sat down beside her cousin.

'Hi, Aunt Joan.'

'Look, sweetheart! I don't want to alarm you, but you had a break-in last night.'

'What?'

'I'm at your place now. The police have just left. Nothing appears to have been taken but the house was ransacked. Please tell me you put the jewellery in a safe place. I went into your bedroom and found the old biscuit tin on the floor, but there was nothing in it.'

Meg looked at Jubilee with alarm.

'It's okay. I put the jewellery in a bank deposit box before I left. They're quite safe.'

'Thank Christ for that. I didn't think for a moment it was kids. They would have taken the television and stereo, yet nothing was taken that I could see. I think someone was looking for that jewellery. How many people have you told?'

'Um ... I've emailed about five jewellers here in England, plus James Hawkins, and a couple of descendants we haven't visited yet,' Jubilee said.

'Well, you need to be careful. Those jewels are obviously worth a lot of money and someone is after them.'

'We will, thanks, Aunt Joan.'

'What about the other paperwork you found, the wallet and photo?' Joan asked.

'I put the wallet in the freezer. I wrapped it in aluminium foil and covered it with 500 grams of mincemeat,' Jubilee said. 'The passport and photo are with me.'

Joan put her iPad down and walked into Jubilee's kitchen. She opened the freezer and saw the frozen plastic bag of mincemeat. She used a knife to remove the frozen meat and found the package inside. Joan opened the wallet and found a key in it.

'It's here, sweetheart,' Joan said, when she returned to the dining table.

Jubilee sighed deeply with relief.

'What's this key doing here?' Joan asked, holding it up for them to see.

'I don't know what it's for. It was hidden in a dog's toy bone. The note in the wallet told me where to find it. I've tried all the locks in and outside the house but nothing remotely fits it.'

'This is a safety deposit box key.'

Both Jubilee and Meg were amazed that Joan knew that instantly.

'The key I have for the deposit box at the National Australia Bank looks nothing like that,' Jubilee said.

'It must be a very old key. Maybe the bank it belongs to has upgraded their deposit boxes since then. If Jack Jones had put something in a deposit box years ago, it must still be there.'

'But which bank?' Meg asked.

They all remained silent as they considered how many banks and branches there were in Bowral and in the entire state of New South Wales for that matter.

'I'll hold onto these for you, Jubilee, unless you want me to post them to you.'

'Thanks, Aunt Joan. You better hold onto them, they're safer with you.'

'Okay. I'll try to figure out which bank this key belongs to. I'll say goodnight and remember to enjoy yourselves. But please be vigilant about what you say and who you talk to in future. Jodie and I will finish tidying the house, and Phil has put an extra lock on the back door and someone is coming tomorrow to replace the windowpane. I've also installed one of those motion sensor cameras outside. I'll know if anyone comes back.'

'I don't think they'll try again, if they didn't find anything the first time.'

'Maybe, but they're tenacious, whoever they are. They've done a lot of damage, I'm afraid you have a number of broken vases and china. A Sergeant Banker came by earlier and introduced himself. He said he was assisting you with your search.'

'Really?' Meg said, a little more enthusiastically. 'Did he say anything else, at all?'

'No. Just that he'd look into the break-in and will organise to have a car drive by each day to check that everything is secure.'

'That's nice of him, don't you think, Jubes?'

Jubilee turned to her cousin and replied emphatically with a big smile.

They both said goodnight to Joan and disconnected the video.

'I can't believe someone broke into your home looking for that jewellery. We've only been here a few days,' Meg said.

'Yes, but I've been emailing jewellers for weeks. What if it's one of them?'

'We can't rule anyone out.'

'Let's be honest, the land might be worth a bit but the house isn't. I'm really pissed off now, someone's trashed my home.'

'Well … someone knows more than they're letting on,' Meg said, sounding concerned. 'Not all of the jewellers we emailed have replied.'

Jubilee decided to change the subject. 'What have you found out about the third robbery at Brunswick House, in Bristol? The current owners are not related to the original owners from 1939.'

'I'm checking on Ancestry,' Meg said. 'The house was sold in 1962, twenty-three years after the robbery. The Brunswick family had lived there from 1755. At the time of the robbery the jewellery that we identified belonged to Emily Brunswick. She had two children. I'm checking through local newspapers and the births, deaths and marriages registry. I've also contacted Helena at the National Archives for information on the family. Hopefully, we'll hear back soon.'

'What about *your* Sergeant Banker? Can he help?'

'I can ask *Billy* to begin a search but he's already co-ordinating with the British police now that we've identified the original owners. Plus, he's also running background checks on Hughie McBean and Tom Fields. He's been very helpful.'

'Okay. I'm looking forward to seeing Amberley Hall tomorrow. We still haven't received a reply to our email.'

'Maybe they think we're scammers too,' Meg said. 'Still, no way to run a business.'

Stepping outside the campervan, Meg folded up the two garden chairs and a small fold-out table and stowed them away. She looked around her at the other campervans and caravans at the site. The school holidays hadn't started yet, but there were still quite a few vans at the campsite. She noticed another campervan with the same markings on its side as theirs. She had seen one similar at the previous campsite. She shrugged and put it down to coincidence as there would be thousands of them touring around England this time of year. Inside the campervan, Meg sat in the driver's seat and drove them out of the campsite and into the town for the evening.

Meg found a parking spot and put money in a parking meter. She didn't notice the black Range Rover that had followed them from the campsite pull up further down the street. A man stepped out and followed them. He stopped at their campervan and scanned the street, noticing four street cameras. He knew now wasn't the time to enter.

He decided to follow them on foot.

Chapter Seventeen

Amberley Hall, Siddington, Cirencester

July 10 – Monday morning – Day 6

*T*he campervan drove through the gates of Amberley Hall a little after 10:00 am.

The grounds were simple and immaculate. In comparison to Bromley House's red brick façade and pristine white window frames, Amberley Hall was straight out of Shakespearean times. The brickwork was partially covered by vines that crawled up the sides of the old house to conceal its ancient appearance and imperfections.

The roof was in disrepair. Like Bromley House, there were windows in the attic, but they were also in need of restoration, including a paint job. The website stated the Hall was over 400 years old, and it visibly looked it.

It didn't go unnoticed that their campervan was the only vehicle in the parking lot, which was located near the side of the house.

'Are you sure they're open today?' Meg asked, looking around for any other visitors.

'Yes, of course. Come on!' Jubilee said, turning off the engine and grabbing her bag. She was feeling grateful not to have a hangover from last night's pub expedition.

Jubilee looked up at the magnificent old house and counted seven chimneys.

Meg was itching to see their library of course, and judging by the age of the house, she hoped the bookshelves still held first edition hard-covered antiques.

They walked towards the side door. A *Welcome* sign stood in front of the entrance. When they entered, they found themselves in a small foyer with a reception desk and a single table selling postcards, cups, tea towels and non-fiction books that pertained to the hall's history.

They rang the reception desk's bell and after a few minutes, an elderly man appeared and shuffled towards them. He sold them two tickets, gave them a map, and explained where they could go and what was out-of-bounds. They were to stay within the marked areas but could walk freely around the grounds. The house and grounds closed at 5:00 pm sharp. Jubilee and Meg thanked him. He shuffled off before they could ask him any questions.

They started their tour on the ground level and entered a stately sitting room. There was an overly large fireplace with ancient furniture surrounding it, which you would have to think twice about before sitting on. The appearance transported them back to the 16th century as Meg tried to imagine what it would have been like. Ladies in their elegant evening gowns, men in their dinner suits, dressing each night for dinner. Horse-drawn carriages to take them wherever they needed to go.

It appeared to Meg that the house hadn't undergone any restorations in decades. Although, if it had been modernised like Bromley House, it would have lost its charm.

However, Jubilee felt a foreboding, as she did in the alley in Plymouth. She was standing in possibly the same room her great-grandfather had stood back in 1939. He came to steal, and possibly forever change the lives of the people living within. Jubilee wondered if the ancient house would have been a modern, stylish and wealthy home today, if not for the robbery.

They made their way through the sad, old house. The furnishings on display were beautiful but there were gaps on the walls where paintings had once hung. Sold over the decades, presumably to pay for its upkeep. As they walked through the dilapidated rooms they felt sorry for the current owners.

Their tour took them into an ancient music room, which led them into the library. Meg was gobsmacked when she saw all the old books on display and was certain some were as old as the house.

'God, would you look at them all. These would fill four bookshops.'

'Don't get romantic on me,' Jubilee said, trying to lead Meg out of the room without much success. Jubilee could see Meg was starting to swoon. If she didn't drag her out soon, she'd have stayed in there all day.

Arriving at a grand old staircase, they walked up to the top but could only turn left as the right side had a partition across the landing. They walked down the corridor and into a couple of stately bedrooms. A four-poster bed nearly hit the ceiling, with elaborate curtains tied up at each of the posts. On their return to the staircase, they could read the sign on the partition: *PRIVATE – DO NOT ENTER.*

Jubilee looked across the landing and saw a large and equally mesmerising portrait of a young man and woman. The woman was sitting with her hands on her lap, while the man stood gallantly beside her with his hand resting on her shoulder.

Jubilee recognised the portrait's background and realised it had been painted in the same music room they just walked out of. Immediately, something else caught her attention.

'Look over there, Meg!' Jubilee pointed to the portrait on the wall. 'Keep a look out. I need a closer look.'

'Alright, but hurry. This place is getting creepy. I feel like I've stepped into *Jane Eyre*.'

Jubilee stepped over the partition and walked across the landing and down the right corridor. She walked up to the portrait and stared longingly at the woman in the picture. It wasn't her beauty that caught Jubilee's eye, although she was beautiful. The jewellery she wore was identical to the tiara and necklace in her biscuit tin.

Jubilee took out her mobile and took a photo of it.

'What are you doing up here?' demanded the voice from across the landing.

Jubilee jumped and spun around to see the old man standing outside a bedroom further down the corridor.

'I'm sorry. I needed a closer look at this portrait.'

'Why?' he demanded.

'My name is Jubilee Jones. Can I please speak with the owners of the hall about this portrait?'

'It isn't for sale.' A flicker of recognition crossed his face at the mention of her name.

'I don't want to buy it. I would like to talk to the owners. Please, it's very important.'

The man glared at Jubilee. He had never grown accustomed to visitors walking around the hall. He wanted her to leave his home, but something about her plea made him agree to speak with her.

'You're the one who emailed about the robbery?' It was more a statement than a question.

'Yes.'

'You better come this way.'

Jubilee and Meg followed the elderly man down the staircase and through the house until they arrived at a door with a plaque on it that said *PRIVATE*. They entered to find a small, pleasant modern sitting room. It was fully furnished and appeared to be well lived-in. There was a fireplace against the far wall, with two settees facing each other adjacent to it. An old armchair was snugly positioned close to the fireplace. A desk rested by a window, which had a computer and printer on it. There were numerous books scattered around the room, from modern best sellers to hard-covered classics, some obviously hand-picked from the library.

The old man invited Jubilee and Meg into the room. A middle-aged woman was resting on a window bench, reading a book. Another man, presumably her husband, was at the desk, typing on the computer. He stood up when he noticed the two strangers standing behind his father.

'This is my son, Jonathan Hardwick and his wife, Emma. I'm William, by the way.' He walked towards the fireplace and sat in his favourite old armchair.

Jubilee introduced themselves.

'How can we help you?' Jonathan asked as he gestured with his hand to Jubilee and Meg to sit on the settee across from his father. He walked over and joined them.

'I was hoping you can tell me who the man and woman are in the portrait on the right-side landing at the top of the staircase. When was it painted?'

'They're my grandparents,' replied Jonathan. 'Thomas and Sofia Hardwick. Why are you interested in the portrait? It isn't for sale.'

'I already told them that,' interrupted William, eyeing the girls, sceptically.

'I was hoping you could tell me about a robbery that took place here in April 1939.'

Jonathan looked a little puzzled. He looked at his father for clarification, who pulled himself forward in his old chair that was worn-in through decades of use.

'Why do you want to know about that?' William asked.

'We may have some information about it.'

'How so?' he replied.

'We've been given copies of the police reports from the National Archives in Kew,' Jubilee began. 'There were five robberies in total within a month of each other. This house was the second in a series of break-ins. I was hoping you might have some documentation relating to what was stolen. Old police reports, jewellery purchase receipts, insurance papers, even diary entries from that time, would be helpful in our search for information.'

'Sofia Hardwick kept a journal for each year of her life,' Emma said, as she stood up and walked over to join them.

Jubilee and Meg turned their attention to Emma as she crossed the room and sat down next to her husband.

They looked at each other a little confused, unsure of Jubilee and Meg's motives.

'Why do you want to know about an 80-year-old robbery?' Jonathan asked.

'She emailed a few days ago asking about it, but I thought she was after something, so I deleted it,' William said.

'We may know who committed the robbery,' Jubilee began, 'but we were hoping you might know something about it.'

Jonathan looked to his wife, who put down her book on the coffee table, and said,

'I typed up Sofia's journals some years ago and printed them collectively into a book. I thought they were beautifully written. Her words were very moving, so I recorded them for posterity. She wrote extensively about that robbery. Her life changed dramatically after that night. They're on display on the table as you walk into the foyer.'

'We'll be sure to buy a copy on our way out. It'll help us with our investigation,' Meg said. 'We're piecing together what happened during and after these robberies. Anything you can tell us about that night would be very helpful.'

'They broke in after midnight,' William said. 'I was only a boy at the time. They came through the servant's entrance. My father attempted to stop them, but he was hurt. He never fully recovered and died four months later. Scotland Yard did come back to say one of the robbers had been killed along a roadside somewhere a few weeks later. I don't remember where. Good riddance, I say. The police never found the other one.'

'I'm so sorry,' Jubilee said, sincerely. She wondered how many more deaths she was going to uncover before her journey was over. William's father's death wasn't in any police report. But as it happened months later, Jubilee guessed they didn't link the two events.

'What happened to your mother and yourself, William?' Meg asked.

'Death duties took most of the money my mother had left. I was the youngest, but as my older brother, Julian was killed in the war, the house fell to me. I've struggled my whole life to keep it up. My mother sold what she could over the years but most of her jewellery was stolen. Unfortunately, a lot of it wasn't insured. My father obviously couldn't afford to insure it. I believe most of her jewellery was family heirlooms, so I couldn't put a price on them now. My mother never got over my father's premature death. Suddenly, she found herself bringing up three children and managing this estate on her own. Everything turned upside down when the war broke out shortly after. In 1943, she received a telegram from the war office informing her that Julian had been killed in action. A part of her died that day.'

Jubilee's tears openly ran down her face. Her journey was becoming more personal each new day. The truth was hard to hear.

'She sold paintings and antique ornaments over the years, whenever she ran out of money – which was often. Unfortunately, my uncle Benjamin arrived about two years after my father's death to help her run the estate. He only came to muscle in on my father's fortune, which there was very little of. He had debts of his own and what money the estate managed to generate he embezzled. In the end, my mother found the courage to throw him out. Most of the land has been sold off now, including most of the valuable artwork and antiques. What you see is what's left. My son, and his endearing wife, Emma,' nodding at his daughter-in-law, 'have been trying to restore it ever since. Regrettably, these houses are money pits. The heating alone runs in the tens of thousands each year. The roof needs repair, and there's damp on the walls, which is why most of the house is shut up.'

'Can I ask why you and your mother chose not to sell?' Meg asked, delicately.

'Because my family is buried here. One of my sisters, Sarah, died of pneumonia in her infancy. My mother wouldn't leave my father or my sister behind, she needed to be near them. This estate was handed down to my father, so my mother felt it was her responsibility to preserve his legacy for his children.'

'But all that will be for nothing now that we'll have to sell,' interrupted Jonathan.

William turned his head to the fireplace and stared into nothing, as no flames crackled in the grate.

'What do you mean?' Jubilee asked.

'We can't keep it afloat any longer,' Jonathan said, looking over at his father. 'I'm a lawyer, and even with my salary, I still couldn't afford to keep it going. We've borrowed to make repairs but I can't put any more debt onto my children. That isn't fair to them. The National Trust has put in an offer. It's reasonable and will clear our debts.'

Meg saw the anguish on William's face. He clearly didn't want to leave his home.

'Why is this all so important to you?' Emma asked. 'What do you know about the robberies?'

Jubilee pulled out her folder from her backpack and began her story.

'About a month ago, back home in Bowral, Australia, I dug up a biscuit tin in my garden. It contained eighteen pieces of jewellery. Meg and I have been trying to piece together who put it there and where it all came from. It appears my great-grandfather wasn't who we thought he was. We believe he was one of the thieves that committed the robbery here in April 1939. The man who was killed along the roadside was Tom Fields, he was a known thief and an associate of a man named Hughie McBean. We think Hughie McBean may have been our great-grandfather. He may also have killed a man in Plymouth and stolen his identity before boarding a ship to Australia. He was known to everyone as Jack Jones.'

The Hardwicks looked at Jubilee and Meg in bewilderment. They were speechless.

Jubilee handed some photos of the jewellery that was inside the biscuit tin. In addition, she handed over a police report itemising the stolen jewellery from Amberley Hall to Jonathan and Emma.

'Good god!' exclaimed Jonathan. He showed one of the pictures to his father.

'As you can see, William, two of those jewellery pieces are worn by your mother in the portrait upstairs on the landing. I have also identified two other pieces belonging to your family, a brooch, and a pair of earrings, which were recorded on the police report. We've come to England to locate their rightful owners.'

William, Jonathan, and Emma were too stunned to comment. William looked at the pictures and began to cry.

'I can't imagine the suffering your mother went through after the robbery,' Meg said, who was becoming as emotional as her cousin. 'We have identified four pieces that belonged to your family. It doesn't account for all that was stolen but we can only assume the thieves divided the jewellery between them and they have possibly been sold long ago.'

'What are you saying? Are you giving us the jewellery back?' William asked.

'Of course. They don't belong to me. They belong to you,' Jubilee said. 'Maybe their current value will be enough to help you keep the hall. If that's what you want.'

William was still looking at the pictures. He was shaking his head.

'Have they been authenticated?' Jonathan asked. The lawyer in him was making it hard to believe what he was hearing. He was a little sceptical.

'I've had one piece authenticated, so I have no reason to believe the other pieces aren't genuine,' Jubilee said. 'The markings on the jewellery have made us believe they're real.

'When we go home, the police will be in contact with you to initiate their return. If you can find any legal documents pertaining to the jewellery, ownership, or purchase receipts, please forward them to us or the police.'

'I'll start searching, Miss Jones,' Jonathan said.

'We don't know what to say,' Emma said, still astonished. 'Thank you.'

'Please don't thank me. The more I discover about my great-grandfather, the more ashamed I am of him. All I can say is, I'm sorry.' Jubilee tried hard to stifle her emotions, she wanted to cry. Meg put her hand on Jubilee's back and rubbed it.

'She's the emotional one,' Meg said, nodding at Jubilee.

They were all overwhelmed. At that point, Jonathan invited Jubilee and Meg to stay for lunch. They closed the hall off to the public, not that they expected anyone else to come and view the ancient hall that day.

Meg handed Jonathan a copy of the police reports. She had made multiple copies for each of the five houses.

During lunch, Jubilee explained what they had uncovered so far, and where they planned to visit next. Emma retrieved one of the books containing Sofia Hardwick's diaries and gave it to Meg.

'Sofia's personality emanates through her journals. I'm sure you'll appreciate her insights after the robbery.'

Meg thanked her.

Emma continued, 'Just after the robbery, Sofia's thoughts had profoundly changed in her diaries. She spoke often about the trauma and aftermath of the attack, along with her husband's death and then, sadly her son's. She struggled emotionally, but only expressed her fears through her journal entries as she didn't want people to know she was unable to cope. Sofia Hardwick was clearly afraid for her children's future.'

Jonathan asked where they were heading next.

'I'm not sure,' Meg said. 'The third house robbed was Brunswick House in Bristol. However, the family no longer live there, so we're trying to trace them.'

'I hope you find them,' William said. 'You've changed our lives and fortunes in a matter of minutes. Hopefully, you can do the same for the others.'

'I hope so,' Jubilee said. She was about to tell them about the break-in back home, but pulled herself up before she did. Jubilee was confident the Hardwicks had nothing to do with it.

Their time with the Hardwicks flew by pleasantly. Jubilee felt no butterflies of guilt or trepidation when it was time to leave.

Returning to the campervan, Jubilee gave Jonathan her personal details and said she would be in touch once they returned to Bowral.

Before climbing into the campervan, Meg turned back to the Hardwicks and collectively said, 'I hope you can find paperwork relating to the jewellery. It will help expedite the transfer.'

Emma promised they would start searching.

William walked up to them. He took Jubilee's face in his shaking hands and kissed her on the cheek. He did the same to Meg.

'Thank you,' was all he managed to say before his emotions got the better of him.

They said their farewells and drove down the short driveway to begin the next leg of their journey towards Bristol. Jubilee hoped Helena, at the National Archives, had discovered something about the descendants of Harold and Emily Brunswick. If not, it would be up to Billy to locate them.

'You know,' Jubilee said, 'I was getting worried. Especially after the break-in back home, but now, I feel that we've actually made a significant difference in someone's life.'

'Yeah, can you imagine how their lives would have been, if not for the robbery?' Meg replied. They both pondered that thought as Jubilee drove out of the main gate and continued their journey south.

Jubilee discretely rubbed her eyes with the cuff of her shirt. She couldn't stop thinking about Meg's last remark. One senseless tragic event had malformed the Hardwicks' lives forever. Was that all it took, for one tragic action to create a chain reaction?

'You bastard, Jack Jones,' she mumbled under her breath, 'or whatever the fuck your name was.' Her thoughts were interrupted by Meg.

'I think we should head on to Grimshaw Manor, in Bath, as we don't have any info on Emily and Harold Brunswick, yet. It might take some time to trace their descendants and we can't wait for days for news as we've already been in England nearly a week. Time is running out for me.'

'Okay. Bath it is,' Jubilee said, then got directions on her phone for Bath.

From Cirencester to Bath took them no more than one and a half hours. They drove through the ancient Roman town of Bath by 4:00 pm.

They booked into a campervan site and both agreed to spend two days sightseeing in Bath while they waited for Helena's reply. There was so much history to be absorbed in Bath and Meg wanted to check out the antique bookshops. She had already accumulated about twenty hard-covered books from her antique bookshop visits, which would need to be shipped home. Driving through the town, they found a parking spot and decided to spend the rest of the day on foot. They hadn't noticed the same black car parked not far from them, which had followed them from Cirencester.

Late that evening, Jubilee cooked them a delicious dinner. Meg opened her laptop and spent a few hours replying to an assortment of emails. Some personal, others were work related. Both women called their mothers to update them on their discovery, although Meg video called her mum to make sure they hadn't burnt down her bookshop. It was mid-morning in Bowral.

'Hi, Mum!'

'Hi, sweetheart! I'm glad you called. I think I know which bank that key belongs to.'

'Really. Which one?'

'The Commonwealth Bank branch on Bong Bong Street. Do you remember what was written on the back of the photo Jubilee had found?'

'Yeah, *Hawthorn Manor, March, 1939*, and something else in the bottom corner.'

'It was *1948 CBBBS*. The number 1948 is for the deposit box number and CB is the Commonwealth Bank, and BBS is Bong Bong Street.'

'Clever clod.'

'I'll go to the bank today and confirm with them if Jack Jones had a deposit box there. I'm a descendent, so I should be able to access what was in the box if I bring identification with me.'

'That's great, mum. Thanks. How's the shop doing?'

'Jodie and I haven't burnt it down yet if that's what you're worried about.'

'Hadn't crossed my mind.'

'Everything is fine here. Take care of yourselves, and I'll call you as soon as I have news about the deposit box.'

'Thanks, Mum. Love ya!'

Meg continued checking her emails and saw there were two from Billy. The first one related to the criminal records of Tom Fields and Hughie McBean. She read out their rap sheets to Jubilee, noting their criminal history was as long as Meg's arm. The second concerned a more sensitive subject which Meg didn't want Jubilee to hear, not until she had read it herself.

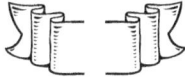

Dear Meg,

Regarding the topic you mentioned below, I had to check with my Inspector before replying as it is a little more complicated than your other requests. In Australia, the legal right to confiscate real property (assets) purchased from the proceeds of crime, is a common occurrence nowadays, especially where drugs and money laundering are involved.

Regarding the ownership of Jubilee's property and, subsequently, that of your mother's home, how can the police determine that the land purchased in 1940 was from the sale of stolen jewellery? If Jack Jones was a long-time criminal, he may have stolen other goods that could have contributed to the purchase of your land. The owners of the missing jewellery would have to prove beyond a doubt that he did. Private individuals cannot commence criminal investigations and are limited to civil proceedings. However, these individuals would also have to consider inheritance laws, which are passed on via probate from the Supreme Court of Australia.

I would surmise it is highly unlikely that the Courts would confiscate Jubilee's property, or your mother's, because of the age of the property, and there is no direct link proving where the money came from to buy it. Who would be able to claim ownership if multiple pieces of jewellery had been sold from different robberies?

There is no statute of limitations when a person can be prosecuted for a criminal offence. Also, considering the age of the offence no one can be held to account today. Please let Jubilee know I believe her home is safe.

How are you going over there? I hope what I've sent you so far is helpful? Please call me next time you need something, as I'd like to hear your voice.

By the way, I deserved that punch on the nose back in art class.

Thinking of you,

Billy.

'Holy crap!' exclaimed Meg.

Meg had a smile on her face the entire time she did the washing up.

Chapter Eighteen

Grimshaw Manor, Bath

July 11 – Tuesday morning – Day 7

Jubilee and Meg arrived at Grimshaw Manor a little after 9:30 am. The driveway was long and impressive. There were no trees lining the driveway, only an immense, perfectly manicured green lawn. The house stood four storeys tall, including the roof, which had small windows protruding from the slated roof. Large windows fanned out across the entire length of the house. Without question, it was the grandest house they had visited so far, but it lacked the warmth of Bromley House. Although it made Amberley Hall look like a poor forgotten relative. Its imposing presence told Meg they wouldn't be welcomed. It reminded her of Rosings Park, in *Pride and Prejudice*. She expected the leering, steely eyes of Lady Catherine de Bourgh to bore down upon her when she entered. Especially considering she was more than two and thirty in age and not married.

'We should've tried to call them first,' Meg said, a little squeamish.

'Are you having second thoughts?'

'I couldn't find their contact number or an email address. They aren't listed in the telephone directory or on Facebook, or any other community platform that I could find,' Meg announced. It appeared they were a very private family.

'Come on. Let's just get it over with,' Jubilee said, feeling somewhat apprehensive herself. They climbed the sixteen steps leading to the front door. Meg walked over to one of the two large rectangular windows on either side of the entrance and stuck her head against the glass and stared inside.

'Oh, crap! We're busted,' she said when she spotted a figure walking through the house towards the door. She quickly moved back beside Jubilee and waited for the door to open.

Jubilee whispered to her cousin, 'I hadn't rung the bell yet. How the hell did they know we were standing here?'

'Two words for you: security cameras,' Meg said, nodding up and towards the left.

The large oak door opened and a woman in her sixties stood in front of them. 'Can I help you?' she said.

'We hope so. We wanted to speak with the owners, Lord and Lady Grimshaw,' Jubilee said.

'They aren't here. They're overseas and won't be back until next week.'

'Damn,' Jubilee said.

'Who is asking?'

'Oh, sorry, my name is Jubilee Jones and this is my cousin, Meg Forrester.'

'Why do you wish to speak with them?' The woman eyed Jubilee and Meg up and down, as if it would help explain their presence.

'I was hoping they could help us regarding an historical robbery that took place here in the late 1930s. We have information relating to the theft of their jewellery.'

The woman's demeanour shifted, but only slightly. She kept her gaze on Jubilee, but she never told them to leave. Jubilee took that as a good sign.

After a long pause, the woman stood aside and allowed Jubilee and Meg to enter. Both women were impressed by the ornately grand entrance hall. In the centre of the foyer was a large staircase that led up to the second level. The steps were made of marble, but the carpet underfoot ensured any footsteps would not echo in the grand room.

The woman led them along a beautiful Calacatta marble floor into a large sitting room, gesturing them to sit. The room's floor was wooden, with lavish rugs beneath regal-coloured furniture. Large portraits adorned the walls and a grand fireplace was prominently displayed in the centre of the room. If it had been ablaze, it would have been magnificent. As Meg took in the room, she tried to imagine herself, snuggled up on the sofa with a good book, while a giant fire crackled in the grate all night. There was a modern portrait of a man and woman, elegantly dressed. Meg assumed they were the current Lord and Lady Grimshaw as she had looked them up online earlier and found a photo taken at a charity event. She was impressed by the likeness.

'My name is Ms Upton, I'm the housekeeper.'

'Thank you for talking with us,' Jubilee said. Once again, she recounted her tale of finding the stolen jewellery. Ms Upton appeared a little incurious, until Meg removed a folder from her bag and showed her the police reports indicating what had been stolen from Grimshaw Manor.

'Are you claiming to have found these pieces?' she asked.

'No, I'm afraid not. There were five robberies in April 1939 but I only have jewellery belonging to four of them,' Jubilee explained.

'So, we're hoping his Lordship could add more light to our research,' Meg said.

'It's most commendable of you but Lord and Lady Grimshaw will not be back until Friday. I'll inform them of your visit. No doubt they will be in touch when they return.'

Ms Upton stood up to indicate their conversation was over.

'Thanks, that's great,' Jubilee said, clearly disappointed. As they were escorted to the door, Meg stopped and asked Ms Upton one final request.

'Is it possible to look at some of the portraits hanging on the walls? I was hoping that some of the jewellery in the police report might be on display. We've been lucky enough to see a couple of portraits showing off the jewellery we've discovered. It would help us immensely with our research.'

'I'm not sure that is appropriate. This is a private residence,' replied Ms Upton.

Meg handed the images of the stolen jewellery to Ms Upton and asked if she recognised any of them.

'Please, what about this one,' Jubilee pleaded, pointing to the diamond necklace made in 1825. She thought Ms Upton was acting colder than the house, although she softened slightly when she looked at the artist's drawing of the diamond necklace. It was inlaid with white gold. Diamonds were patterned along its curvature and formed a delicate pattern of a bird's wings.

'Well ... I do recognise this,' she said. Jubilee and Meg could see she was warming to the idea. 'I'll have to accompany you, but I can't see that it would hurt. Please follow me.'

'Absolutely,' Jubilee said.

She turned from them and headed out of the room. Jubilee and Meg dutifully followed Ms Upton in silence.

Walking through the manor, they passed many portraits and landscapes, but neither one recognised any of the jewellery from the police report.

Ms Upton took them up the grand staircase and along a corridor. They entered a bedroom that appeared straight out of a Jane Austen novel. There was a large four-poster bed with delicate shear fabric tied up on each corner of the poster bed. It was twice as big as Jubilee's bed at home. The cabinets and dressing table were centuries old, and still in immaculate condition. There was a large ewer and bowl sitting on the dressing table.

Ms Upton walked over to the fireplace. Above it was a portrait of a young woman. Ms Upton had admired this portrait for decades. It held a personal affection for her.

'This is a portrait of Lady Jane Grimshaw. The diamond necklace was a gift from her father on her wedding day. It had belonged to her great-grandmother.'

All three stared at the beautiful young woman in the portrait. Her beauty was only matched by the elegance of the diamond necklace and matching earrings. Her hair was in the style of the times, it was plaited at the sides and pulled back into an elegant bun. Resting on her head was a delicate tiara. They had to commend the artist, if it was indeed a genuine likeness, then she was truly beautiful.

'It's stunning,' Meg said in awe, although her attention was on the necklace and tiara.

'Lady Jane doesn't look very old in that picture,' Jubilee remarked.

'No. I believe she was seventeen years old when she married. It's quite sad, actually.'

'How so?' Jubilee asked, dreading another ill-fated story that her great-grandfather was accountable for.

'I'm sorry, I shouldn't have said that.'

'Why not? This all happened nearly a century ago. What does it matter now?' Meg said.

Ms Upton considered her position.

'I guess not. The marriage wasn't a happy one. You have to understand in those days, young women of her calibre, were expected to marry well to preserve their family's wealth or marry into it. They were merely pawns on a chessboard.'

'You mean, blue bloods marrying blue bloods,' Meg said, indelicately.

'Yes. If you want to put it that way. I believe she was trapped in a loveless marriage. Lord Robert Grimshaw was much older than Lady Jane. Nonetheless, she was blessed with three children that she adored. But, sadly, on the day of her thirtieth birthday, in September 1941, she was found drowned in the lake. You can see it from her bedroom window there.' Ms Upton nodded towards the window. 'The police ruled it an accidental drowning.'

'How sad,' Jubilee replied.

'You said she had three children. Presumably, the estate would have gone to the oldest son?' Meg asked.

'Lady Grimshaw's personal affairs are none of my business. Or yours, for that matter.'

'I just mean,' Meg said, rephrasing, 'if we had found any jewellery belonging to the Grimshaws we would need to speak with the ancestor who would have inherited it.'

'I'm sorry, but you'll need to speak with my employer regarding their financial matters.'

'We would if they were here,' Meg said, a little put out.

While Meg and Ms Upton talked, Jubilee walked over to the window and looked out across the garden which spanned over ten acres. She stared down at the placid lake. She felt a sense of dread build up inside her. Thinking how sad Lady Jane must have been to live in an unhappy marriage in such a beautiful and tranquil place. Her children would have been devastated. With her arms crossed, she absent-mindedly twirled her ring around her finger.

Jubilee turned away from the window and asked Ms Upton another question. 'Did Lady Jane ever keep a journal or diary that you know of?'

There was a moment's pause before she replied, 'I can't say.' The question clearly took Ms Upton by surprise. This didn't go unnoticed by either cousin.

'Can't or won't?' Meg asked.

'Even if there were, I doubt Lord Giles and Lady Joanna Grimshaw would allow you to see them. They are a private family.'

'I'm sorry. My cousin didn't mean to offend you. Did you Meg?' Jubilee glared at Meg to apologise.

'Sorry. We've come a long way and we're searching for answers. We have witness statements and police reports, but first-hand accounts are more personal.'

Ms Upton said she couldn't help them but would pass on their request to her employer. She escorted Jubilee and Meg along the corridor and down the oversize staircase back to the front entrance. She said they would be in touch.

Meg stopped at the door and turned to face Ms Upton. 'One more thing. How long have you been the housekeeper here?'

Ms Upton saw no reason to hide that fact. 'I've worked here for over forty years.'

'Did you know who the housekeeper was before you?'

'Yes. My mother and my father had been the head gardener.'

'Would your mother remember anything from 1939 including Jane's death?' Meg asked.

'You mean Lady Grimshaw's death.'

'Yeah, sorry.' Meg was forgetting protocol.

'No. She died ten years ago.'

'I'm sorry,' Meg said, honestly.

Jubilee and Meg climbed back into the campervan, mutually feeling disappointed. They were both silent for a while until Jubilee broke it.

'You were harsh on Ms Upton, Meg.'

'She lied to us. Most women like Lady Jane would have kept a diary at some point in their lives, if not throughout their lives. It would have been her only outlet to escape her miserable existence here.'

'Maybe she doesn't believe it's our business.'

'Well, I for one would like to know what Lady Jane was thinking prior to her death. Don't you find that a bit suspicious, she drowned in her own lake? Why would she have gone in there at that time of the year? It would've been freezing.'

Jubilee had thought the same thing. Maybe, she was trying to save one of her children? Jubilee wondered if Billy could request the police report into Lady Jane's death. But she quickly shook the thought away, she was overreacting. This wasn't the reason why she was here in England. Tragedies happen in life.

'We can't hang around until Friday waiting for his Lordship to return. We may have to leave them till last,' Meg said.

'Agreed,' Jubilee replied, snapping out of her deliberations.

Meg started the campervan and headed down the long driveway.

*   *   *

Ms Upton had watched for a long time after the two women drove away. Old memories slowly resurfaced. Her mother had been a discreet and loyal housekeeper. It wasn't until her last few days that she had finally opened up and told her the truth about Lady Jane.

Ms Upton stood at the front door wondering if this encounter was a sign. Was it now time for justice to be done?

Ms Upton went to her private quarters below stairs. She reached under her bed and retrieved a suitcase. She opened it and removed a brown envelope. Sitting motionless on her bed for some time, she tried to comprehend what she should do. She had dreaded the day when her mother's secret would resurface.

Mabel had given her daughter an envelope containing a diary and a letter from Lady Jane prior to her death. She was instructed to keep it safe.

Ms Upton didn't need to open the letter. She knew it, word for word.

The letter simply said –

Dear Mabel,

Keep my diary safe and let justice be done.

Mabel Upton had been too afraid to do anything about the diary, except keep it safe. The war never seemed to end, and when it did, jobs were scarce. Years later, Mabel married Owen, the head gardener, and remained at the manor most of her life. She saw no reason to bite the hand that feeds.

Mabel's decision had caused her great regret. On her deathbed, she told her daughter, 'loyalty works both ways.'

Chapter Nineteen

Bath

July 11 – Tuesday mid-afternoon

After lunch, Jubilee and Meg decided to take themselves off for a lengthy walk. They parked the campervan in the city down a side street and then began the Bath Skyline Walk. They'd packed their backpacks with food and drink, not forgetting their phones and wallets. Meg had packed her iPad, preferring to take panoramic photos on it rather than from her mobile. They trekked through meadows and woodlands for miles. The fresh air helped clear the cobwebs from their minds. They still had two families to meet, and Jubilee was apprehensive about uncovering more family tragedies.

It turned out to be a glorious day. Nothing appeared to stop the cousins from enjoying their time in the ancient Roman town of Bath. Jubilee and Meg were nostalgic for the old buildings, monuments, and churches. England's history appeared endless; no buildings back home were more than 250 years old. Australia was still in the process of writing its own history.

The day passed quickly, but when they returned to their campervan a little after 5:00 pm, they were shocked to discover the campervan's door was slightly ajar. Meg knew she locked it before they went out.

Meg cautiously opened the door and stepped inside. She couldn't believe what she was seeing. The campervan had been ransacked. Food and kitchen utensils were scattered all over the bench and floor. Clothes were thrown everywhere. It was hard to tell if anything was missing, but Meg was furious at the violation.

Meg inspected the lock and could see it had been jimmied. She pulled out her mobile and took photos, then called the police.

'This can't be a coincidence, Meg.'

'No. Someone was looking for something. As if we'd keep the bloody jewellery in the campervan.'

'Check our passports, Meg,' Jubilee said, angrily.

Meg quickly pulled out the bedside drawer. She sighed with relief when she saw their passports were still there, along with Jack Jones's passport and picture. Meg picked them up and waved them at her cousin.

'Where's my computer?'

Jubilee rummaged through the mess but couldn't locate her computer. Meg quickly did the same. Swearing out loud, Jubilee sat on the bed and cried with frustration. Her folder containing all her research was missing.

'Well, I guess they found what they were looking for, whoever they are,' sighed Jubilee.

'Please tell me you backed everything up to the cloud after our visit to Grimshaw Manor,' Meg said, frozen, unable to move until her cousin confirmed she had.

'Yeah, thank god, I did it while you drove into town.'

'Maybe the police can check street cameras and take fingerprints. This isn't a coincidence,' Jubilee said, bending down to pick up her underwear.

'Well now I'm pissed off. What the hell's going on? We're giving the jewellery back, so there's no need for this.'

Jubilee looked around the dishevelled campervan. All their clothes were scattered on the floor, mingled in with all their food products, which now would all need to be washed.

Before the police's arrival, Jubilee and Meg had agreed not to mention the robberies and their reason for coming to England. When the police finally arrived, they said they would check for CCTV cameras. Regrettably, as they were parked on a side street, they might be out of luck. The police agreed to dust for fingerprints but alluded to the break-in as probably kids, otherwise their passports would have been taken.

Jubilee and Meg waited outside until forensics had finished their sweep. The police gave them an incident report number to claim on their travel insurance. Before leaving, the police told Jubilee and Meg to call a locksmith and fix the lock on their campervan door, and to hand the police report to the campervan hire company so they could receive a refund for the costs incurred.

Later that night, they drove to a new campervan site and spent the rest of the night tidying up. Jubilee scrubbed down every surface with disinfectant, while Meg put everything back where it belonged. They put their clothes into a bag for washing and once they were finished cleaning, they sat exhausted at the table. Meg finally admitted the obvious.

'Maybe we've stumbled upon something more than just stolen jewellery. Someone knows more than they're letting on or they think we know more than we're letting on,' Meg said. Seeing how upset Jubilee was, she conceded, 'we were bound to ruffle a few feathers along the way. Don't take it personally.'

'Wasn't that your work laptop?'

'Good god, no! I wouldn't have brought that with me. It was my old one. I was checking my emails in the browser, so they won't be able to see those or anything else, it's all password protected. If they're that determined, they could find someone to hack in.'

'Do we have anything that secretive?'

'I'll reset my passwords just to be on the safe side.'

Jubilee sat defeated at the little table, she was having second thoughts about her adventure. She was getting an uneasy feeling that she would make matters worse.

Meg could see Jubilee's demeanour change. 'Don't let them intimidate you. You can get a new computer tomorrow, and we can reprint what was in the folder. It's just a setback that's all. But for tonight, you'll have to use my iPad or your mobile to do further research.'

'Great …' Jubilee felt demoralised.

'It could have been worse, Jubes.'

'I just feel violated, you know? They even pulled out my underwear.'

Meg giggled, 'At least they were clean.'

Jubilee looked at Meg, knowing it was a laugh or cry moment. She desperately wanted to cry, but they laughed instead.

Meg logged onto Ancestry using her iPad. She checked for any new links to the Brunswick family who once lived at Sandalwood Lodge, Bristol. As yet no luck. She logged out and signed into her inbox and saw an email from Helena at the National Archives.

'Hey, Jubes. We have a reply from Helena.' Jubilee got up and sat down beside Meg, as she read the message aloud.

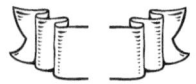

Dear Meg and Jubilee,

I hope your search is going well. I have the pleasure of informing you that I have found a number of records concerning the descendants of Emily and Harold Brunswick of Sandalwood Lodge.

Please see attached my findings.

If there is anything else I can help you with further, please don't hesitate to contact me.

Yours sincerely,

Helena Lee.

There were six file attachments. Meg opened the first document containing a family tree.

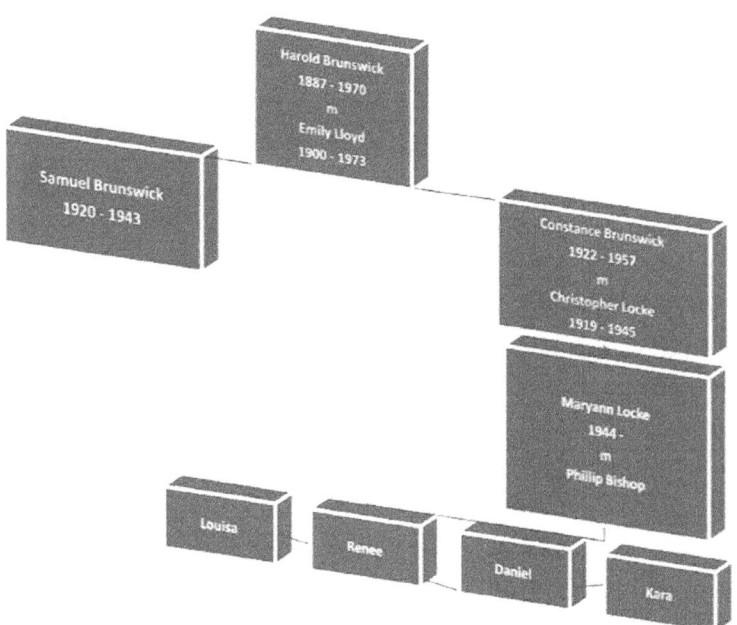

It began with Emily and Harold Brunswick. They had two children, Samuel and Constance. Samuel had no wife or children below his name. When Meg opened the second attachment, it was from the War Office. It was a notification of Samuel Brunswick's death, killed in action, in 1943.

The third attachment was a marriage certificate of Constance Brunswick to Christopher Locke and a birth certificate for a daughter named Maryann Locke.

The fourth attachment were two death certificates. The first certificate stated Christopher Locke was killed in action in 1945. The second certificate was issued for Constance Locke who died in 1957 of influenza.

The fifth attachment was a document relating to Maryann Locke, who was placed in an orphanage at the age of thirteen after her mother's death in 1957.

The final document was the marriage certificate of Maryann Locke, to Phillip Bishop, in 1966.

'Oh, thank Christ, for that!' Meg sighed. 'I thought it was going to say Maryann died as well.'

Maryanne's family tree listed four children, Louisa, Renee, Daniel, and Kara.

Both women rolled their eyes with relief.

'I'm so pleased we've found them,' Jubilee said. 'They won't be hard to trace now.'

'Why was Maryann put in an orphanage when she had a stately home to live in with her grandparents?'

'Good question. Let's find out. When did her grandparents die?'

Meg viewed the Brunswick family tree again.

'It says Emily Brunswick died in 1973, while Harold Brunswick died in 1970. Did Constance not inherit?' Meg was puzzled. 'I read earlier that the house was sold in 1962.'

'Do you want me to start searching for the children of Maryann Bishop?' Jubilee asked, not so enthusiastically.

'No, I'll do it. I know you secretly hate searching for anything on the internet. You suck at it anyway. I'll do the searches.'

Relieved, Jubilee checked her inbox for any new emails. 'Hang on, I have an email from Alex Everett.'

'What does she want?' Meg asked. It was Jubilee's turn to read aloud the email from Alex.

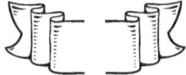

Dear Jubilee,

How is your search going? Have you identified the descendants of the jewellery you discovered?

It hasn't taken long for word to spread around town of your discovery.

May I give you a word of advice? Do not give the Flame of India to the Henley-Smiths. I am referring to the ruby set you have found. I believe the robbery was an inside job, perpetrated by the Henley-Smiths themselves. The police will need to be involved before any distribution of the jewellery takes place.

There is much more to these robberies than you might realise. All I can say for now is to be very careful. People will go to great lengths to protect their reputations.

Yours sincerely,

Alex Everett

Starr and Everett

'Well, that's interesting. At least we now know it's named the Flame of India. How would someone know that it was an inside job, unless they were a part of it?' Meg asked. 'There's nothing in the police report insinuating that, we only have Starr and Everett stating it.'

'It might be true, the robberies weren't investigated after the war, remember. I'm more interested to know why she's so keen for us not to hand the jewellery back, especially when we know who it belongs to?'

Jubilee wondered if Alex Everett had something to do with the break-ins at home and their campervan. It also hadn't gone unnoticed that it was Starr and Everett who made the ruby set.

Meg told Jubilee to send a reply to Alex thanking her for her thoughtfulness. But told her not to give anything away. It was time they had some answers of their own.

Meg spent the remainder of the night on the iPad, making great progress in between glasses of Chardonnay. She found the Facebook profile of Renee Gardener – daughter of Maryann Bishop. It was a quarter to twelve when Meg sent Renee Gardener a message request. She hoped Renee would be open enough to answer a stranger's request.

Jubilee spent the evening reading Sofia Hardwick's diaries.

*   *   *

July 12 – Wednesday morning – Day 8

Jubilee and Meg agreed to spend the day shopping and sightseeing. They promised themselves it wouldn't be all work and no play. They strategically chose a parking spot across the road from the Bath Police Station for added measure. They visited the Roman Baths, and Bath Abbey. Afterwards, they had lunch in Alexandria Park and walked along The Circus, Bath's most famous street. They browsed through more bookshops, longer than Jubilee would have liked. Finally, Jubilee pleaded with Meg to find a cafe, as she desperately needed a coffee.

Jubilee had purchased a new laptop and once inside the cafe, Meg helped Jubilee set it up. They had purchased a new folder and would later find a print shop and print off their stolen research.

While in the cafe, Meg added more pictures to her Facebook profile, while Jubilee emailed pictures directly to her mother on her phone.

They still hadn't received any news from Joan back in Bowral about the bank deposit key. It was now a waiting game.

'Oh, Jubes. I've got a message from Renee Gardener.'

Jubilee put down her cup and licked her lips to remove the milk froth. 'Go on then. What does she say?'

Meg read it out:

Are you a friend of my mother? Why are you asking about her?

Jubilee told Meg she should ask Renee about Sandalwood Lodge only. 'If we text her about stolen jewellery, she won't reply.'

'I'll say I'm researching Sandalwood Lodge,' Meg said, 'cataloguing its history and would like to know about the Brunswick family. Can we discuss over the phone, or can we meet in person?'

'Good. What if she doesn't know she's related to them?' Jubilee asked.

'It wasn't hard for us to trace their family. I'd dare say someone in her family must have traced theirs over the years. If not, then they're in for a big surprise,' Meg said.

'Okay, but Maryann Bishop is still alive, she must know who her grandparents are.'

'We clearly didn't.'

'Point taken. Let's just see what reply we get.'

Meg replied to Renee Gardener, hoping she was a curious individual.

'You know, Maryann may not want to talk about it. If she was put in an orphanage, there must have been bad blood between them.'

'Maybe, they were too elderly or too infirm to look after her,' Jubilee added.

They waited another twenty minutes before receiving Renee's reply.

I spoke with my mother. She has agreed to speak with you. We can meet tomorrow in Clevedon at a cafe called Tiffin at the Beach, at 10:00 am.

Meg and Jubilee finished their coffees and walked back to their campervan. They rested for an hour before heading towards Bristol and the town of Clevedon. They found another campsite about six miles outside of Clevedon. They enjoyed a quiet night in at the campervan site, still a little too anxious to leave the campervan unattended.

*   *   *

It was a little after 10:00 pm when Joan sent Meg a text to call her, as she sat in front of her iPad and waited for her daughter to reply. Within five minutes, they were talking on a video call.

'So, what happened, please don't keep us in suspense?' Jubilee pleaded.

'I have good news and bad, sweetheart,' was Joan's first remark. 'Jack did have a safety deposit box at the Commonwealth Bank, on Bong Bong Street.'

'Wow, the sneaky bastard,' Jubilee said.

'Agreed. Unfortunately, it isn't there anymore. I had to fill in a lot of paperwork before they could tell me anything. After Jack died, the rent on the deposit box lapsed. Your great-grandmother mustn't have known anything about it, or if she did, she wasn't interested. After a few years, the bank handed the contents of the box over to the state. It's called escheatment.'

'So, where's it now?' Meg asked.

'I don't know. The bank said it would be with either the Treasurer or the Unclaimed Property Office. I've been in contact with both of them and they've sent me forms upon forms to fill in. I'll send them off today, so hopefully we'll finally have some answers.'

'Thanks for all your help, Aunt Joan. We really appreciate it.'

'You can thank your uncle for that, he helped with the mounds of paperwork. You've got me all intrigued now, Jubilee. How are you both getting on?'

'We've spoken to two families so far, and we're off to speak to Maryann Bishop and her daughter, Renee Gardener, tomorrow.'

'That's great. I hope it isn't all business. Where are you now?'

'Clevedon near Bristol,' Meg said.

'Is everything alright over there?'

Meg looked at Jubilee, her gesture implied not to mention the break-in.

Jubilee said they were going great and thanked Joan once again before saying goodnight, while Meg continued to chat with her mum a bit longer. After saying goodnight, Meg spent the evening snuggled up in bed, reading a new book.

They only had seven days left to discover the truth.

Jubilee had a restless night. Her thoughts kept circling around safety deposit boxes and her underwear. Would the deposit box contain the remainder of the missing jewellery?

That was her obvious choice. Her thoughts were sketchy and fractured. Where would she end up when this was all over? It was becoming less clear each day. She had fleeting images of standing in a commercial kitchen, barking orders at her staff. Where was she? Owning her own restaurant was every chef's dream, so why was she rattled? Where did she belong?

Jubilee eventually fell asleep in the early hours of the morning. Time was escaping her.

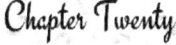

Chapter Twenty

Clevedon

July 13 – Thursday morning – Day 9

Jubilee and Meg parked along the promenade overlooking the Bristol Channel. It was supposed to be summer, however, when they stepped out of the campervan the cold wind hadn't figured that out yet. It whipped across their faces, like a sharp slap.

Grudgingly, Meg was persuaded to take a walk along Clevedon Pier. Then they went back down the street until they found the Tiffin at the Beach cafe.

'I think my nose has frozen,' Meg said, rubbing it with her mittens.

'Stop complaining, the cold sea air will clear your sinuses,' Jubilee said.

'I don't have sinuses, only frostbite. I think my snot has frozen!' Meg exclaimed, as they entered the cafe.

Meg and Jubilee found a table inside, positioned against the far wall and took off their outer layers. They ordered a hot drink while they waited for their guests to arrive.

They only had to wait another fifteen minutes before Renee Gardener entered the cafe with her mother, Maryann Bishop. Meg identified Renee from her Facebook profile and waved.

As their guests approached, Jubilee and Meg stood up and introduced themselves.

'Thank you so much for coming. I know our request seemed strange, but there is more to this than we told you,' Meg said.

'I don't understand. I thought this was about Sandalwood Lodge?' Renee asked, confused.

'Yes, it is – in part. My cousin simply means that we didn't want to scare you off by disclosing everything all at once.'

It seemed Renee wanted to leave, but Maryann spoke up, saying, 'We're here now love, let's hear them out. I'm gasping for a cup of tea.'

Renee nodded, and they seated themselves across from Jubilee and Meg.

Jubilee and Meg told them where they were from. They ordered a fresh round of tea and coffee. Jubilee took her folder from her bag, ready to present her findings about Sandalwood Lodge and the robbery.

'We know that Emily Brunswick lived at Sandalwood Lodge up until 1962, up until it was sold,' Jubilee began. 'We hope this isn't too personal, but we need to understand why Constance Brunswick didn't inherit the estate, following her brother's death during the war.'

Maryann took a gulp of her tea and gently placed the cup back on the saucer.

'Well my dear, my grandparents didn't approve of the man my mother married. You see, Constance became a nurse during the war. She met my father, Christopher Locke, during his convalescence at a rehabilitation centre, recovering from his wounds. They fell in love, as many did during the war. My grandparents disapproved of Christopher Locke and wouldn't give their blessing. They saw him as a commoner, someone below their station, if you know what I mean. She chose love over duty, so they cut her off and refused to see her again. My father was killed in action on August 3, 1945, a month before the end of the war.'

'I'm so sorry,' Jubilee said, feeling uneasy about what Maryann was going to say next.

'It was all a long time ago. The past is best left where it belongs,' Maryann said.

Jubilee smiled at Maryann's phrase, which reminded her of her mother. But she had to ask, 'What happened to you?'

Maryann paused before continuing, 'My mother and I carried on after the war like most people. It was a struggle but we managed because she was a trained nurse. Then, she fell ill and died of influenza in 1957. I knew of my grandmother, as I met her once. My mother had asked her for help, but she wouldn't, or couldn't give it. My grandfather was a very strict and unforgiving man, and after my mother's death, I was put in an orphanage in Bristol. I was well cared for, and when I was sixteen I got a job. I got on with my life. I met Phillip Bishop when I was nineteen and we've been happily married ever since.'

'Do you know what happened to Sandalwood Lodge?' Meg asked. 'Why was it sold?'

'Emily Brunswick sold the estate in 1962,' Renee said, placing her hand on her mother's arm. 'It was in disrepair and she couldn't afford to keep it up anymore. Harold was placed in a nursing home and died in 1970. Emily Brunswick contacted my mum once Harold was deposited in the home. She expressed regret for not taking my mother in after my grandmother's death. But as far as I'm concerned, it was too little too late.'

Jubilee and Meg could sense Renee's anger and animosity towards her great-grandmother, Emily Brunswick. She held contempt and despised Emily's weakness of character for not helping her daughter and granddaughter when they needed her the most.

'Blood is blood,' Renee said. 'They should have cared for both of you. Their prejudice was no excuse for abandoning you. He was cruel and she was weak, they deserved to be lonely. My mum's amazing, unfortunately, I'm not as forgiving.' Renee looked at her mum.

Maryann squeezed her daughter's hand and smiled lovingly at her. Jubilee silently agreed with Renee. Stubborn pride had cost Emily and Harold Brunswick a daughter and grandchild's love. Jubilee felt no pity for them.

'Did you inherit anything from Emily Brunswick? I don't mean to be intrusive but I need to ask,' Jubilee said.

'When my grandmother died, her estate left me a little money, trinkets, and some family photos,' Maryann said. 'I believe she rented after leaving Brunswick House and died alone and unloved. It's very sad, but I forgave her. Although, my daughter has not.'

'Well, we have some interesting news to share with you,' Jubilee began. 'It's a long story, so perhaps we should order another round of tea and some cakes.'

Jubilee recounted her story about the fateful biscuit tin and concluded by showing Renee and Maryann the police report detailing the five estates robbed, and an itemised list of what was stolen from Sandalwood Lodge.

'Well, I'll be,' Maryann said.

'Serves them right,' Renee chuckled.

'That's why we're here in England, to return the jewellery to its rightful owners. So, you know what that means, don't you?'

Jubilee looked at Maryann and Renee. They didn't quite register what she was saying. 'If you're the sole descendant of Harold and Emily Brunswick, and she left you the remainder of her estate, then the jewellery should be transferred to you, Maryann.'

'We don't have all the items,' Meg said. 'However, we found a third of what was stolen.' Meg presented them with a photocopy of the pendant, detailing the cross, made from silver and adorned with diamond-patterned gems. 'There was a diamond necklace made of white gold, with matching earrings, and a ring. Plus there were two other rings that appeared to be family heirlooms based on their age.'

Jubilee informed them, 'These now belong to you. The jeweller who made the necklace has valued it well over £200,000.'

Both women remained speechless.

'And you're just going to hand them over?' Renee asked, a little sceptical.

'Yes. We'll inform the police, and if you have any legal documents relating to Emily Brunswick's will, you'll need to give them to the police. If not, you can obtain them from her solicitor. When we return home, we'll arrange for your jewellery to be returned to you. You can keep or sell them, it's up to you.'

Both women exchanged bewildered glances while reviewing the reports from Scotland Yard on the Sandalwood Lodge robbery.

Knowing it highly unlikely, Jubilee asked, 'I don't suppose Emily Brunswick ever mentioned anything about a robbery in 1939 when you spoke with her?'

'No,' Maryann said, 'she didn't.'

'Well Mum, I guess your grandparents left you something to remember them by after all,' Renee said, laughing. 'Whether they wanted to or not.'

'I don't know what to say …' Maryann started to say more, but a tear caused her to stop.

The four women chatted about their lives for an additional hour at the cafe. It was as if they were old friends reunited and when it came time to leave, Maryann was lost for words. Before they parted, she kissed Jubilee and Meg on their cheeks. Renee thanked Jubilee and Meg once more, promising to stay in touch. Renee knew her mother wouldn't keep the jewellery. She had no need for fancy trinkets, but she did have many children and grandchildren she wanted to help.

*   *   *

Feeling a sense of gratification, Jubilee and Meg took another long stroll down the promenade. The wind had abated and the breeze was refreshing. It was turning into another pleasant day. They found a seat and relaxed as they enjoyed the sea view.

Jubilee smiled outwardly, and said, 'I think we've really made a difference here today. Don't you agree?'

'Today's been a good day, and before you say, "I know," you don't know. You've always carried the weight of the world on your shoulders. You blamed yourself when your dad bunked off, but it was never about you, he was just an asshole. You even blamed yourself that your mum never married until Marcus came along. But again, that was your mum's choice.'

'What's your point?'

'My point is that you always take things to heart. What Jack Jones did was on him. Not you, nor me, nor anyone else. You're simply retelling his story.'

Jubilee smiled at her cousin, she always knew what to say. 'It just amazes me though how a single action can have such a profound impact on so many lives. Look at me now, if it hadn't been for COVID, I'd still be in Sydney. I love being a chef – I do, but I felt like I was standing in quicksand. Do you understand what I mean?'

'Of course I do. We all get that way sometimes. Don't forget how worried I was about losing my bookshop. If it was in Sydney, I would have undoubtedly faced closure,' Meg said, remembering those tough years. Fortunately, Bowral's restrictions weren't as severe as Sydney's. With people stuck at home with nowhere to go, they chose to read and cook, so she survived it. A little worse for wear but still standing. Despite minimal foot traffic, her online orders increased by 300%, which was crucial for her survival. 'The worst part really was how lonely I was when the bookshop shut. I didn't want to return home to Mittagong because people still wanted to buy books. Before then, many locals would come in and browse and chat or simply buy a coffee and read for a while. I knew all my regulars by their first names and remember how my book clubs and poetry nights had to go online for a year? Most people don't like change, so it was a challenge to adapt. Everyone needs companionship in one way or another.'

'I didn't know you felt that way.'

'We've both experienced heartbreak, Jubes, only I don't like to talk about it,' Meg said. 'You know, out of all that mess we discovered a new way of living, and for the most part, we coped. We adapted, like all creatures do to a changing environment. If it wasn't for wi-fi and the internet, nobody would have been able to work from home. Some people have been even more productive that way. Less travel costs and no sitting in traffic for an hour each morning and night. That would have been unimaginable a decade or two ago.'

'You're right,' Jubilee remarked, 'but if we're adaptable creatures, why can't we learn from our mistakes?'

Meg chuckled at her cousin, 'You'll be alright. You'll find your place in this world, once you determine what you really want from it. You need to believe you deserve it.'

Jubilee placed her hand on Meg's and gave it a gentle pat. Their bond was so strong – whenever Jubilee needed a pep talk, it was always Meg whom she could confide in. She had missed that connection while living in Sydney.

Their final destination was Harrowgate Hall, in Bridgewater, Somerset. They decided to head down to Somerset that same afternoon. It wasn't a lengthy journey. They had yet to receive a reply from the housekeeper, Ms Upton, or Lord and Lady Grimshaw, at the Manor.

'Sir Rupert Henley-Smith the third has finally sent an email indicating he would allocate us half an hour. Shall we visit this afternoon?' Meg asked, with a grin.

'Absolutely,' Jubilee replied with a cheeky grin, 'now you're talking.'

Chapter Twenty One

Hatton Garden

'They called the police.'

'Did anyone see you?' Louis Blackman asked.

'No. I was careful and I couldn't see any surveillance cameras on the streets. I took their computers along with a folder that contained all their documents. I arranged the break-in to look like kids had done it.'

'Bring the computers to me. We'll see what's on them.'

'Will do.'

Louis hung up on his associate. He couldn't take any chances, not if the two Australian women knew more than they were letting on. They had to know the whereabouts of the remaining jewellery. The stones couldn't all have been sold, not without attracting attention. He knew gold and silver could be melted down, but stones of that calibre weren't as easily shifted. If the remaining jewellery was still hidden, someone must know its location. Louis had known about McBean's reputation. He wasn't the kind of thief to let sleeping dogs lie. He would want revenge for Tommy and he would have hidden any evidence for insurance.

Louis sat quietly in his office as he contemplated his next move. His grandfather and father both possessed a skill and quality of character that enabled them to break down stolen jewellery and re-design it into exquisite original masterpieces. After all, that's how the company made its wealth. However, Louis never possessed that artistic skill, so he improvised and found other ways to make his fortune. He chose to become a diamond merchant, focusing his talents on trading in quality gems and anything else he could get his hands on. The last thing he wanted was for anyone to dig up the past. However, Giles Grimshaw would be calling soon. Louis doubted he would hold his nerve.

His firm would get through this, as long as no one talked.

*   *   *

Arriving in Bridgewater later that afternoon, the map on Meg's phone directed them to Harrowgate Hall. Jubilee drove down a long private road with Italian cypress trees lining both sides of the gravel driveway. They performed like soldiers on parade, poised for the general's inspection. The hall was an impressive sight. The main building was three storeys high, with single-storey additions stretched out on either side. To the right, the single-storey addition was dwarfed by a huge oak tree. It was clearly older than the hall. Giant windows spanned the length of the building designed to capture an abundance of sunlight.

Jubilee and Meg tidied themselves up before exiting their campervan. They walked up to the front door and pressed the doorbell.

After a three-minute delay, it was answered by the butler.

'May I help you?' he asked.

Jubilee stepped forward. 'Ah, yes. We would like to speak with Sir Rupert Henley-Smith, the third.'

'Or the fourth?' Meg asked, raising an eyebrow. 'We're expected.'

The butler scrutinised them briefly before allowing them admittance. He escorted them directly to the library. Predictably, Meg was overwhelmed by the enormity of the room and the thousands of books paraded on the shelves. The entire room was covered from floor to ceiling with shelves, lined with hard-covered books. Meg spun around, unsure where to look first.

The butler instructed them to wait there while he spoke with the master of the house. Meg told him to take his time as she began to explore the room. She stopped in front of one particular book.

'Christ, Jubes. This is a first edition. It's by …'

'Don't touch anything. It's probably worth more than our lives,' Jubilee cautioned.

'Oh my god. Look at this one.'

Jubilee could see her cousin was back in love again. Her love affairs were often fleeting romances, as she dallied from one author to another.

Before Jubilee could reply, the door swung open to reveal an elderly man.

'Good afternoon. I am Sir Rupert Henley-Smith. Who are you and why are you asking about an historic robbery?'

He wasn't a man to be trifled with. He promptly took control of the situation, making it clear to Jubilee and Meg that they were under scrutiny.

'We have some information about the robbery we emailed you about, and were hoping you could add additional information to what we already know,' Jubilee said.

He hesitated a moment, eyeing them with a frigid stare before he spoke frankly. 'The theft happened on April 28, 1939. The thieves were never caught, except one, who was later found dead along a road, killed by his own partner no doubt. I dare say they quarrelled over the dividend, like vultures.'

'Yeah ... okay,' Meg said, surprised by his bluntness. 'Can you confirm what was stolen?'

'Not until you tell me why you're asking about a century-old robbery.'

'I dug up some of your stolen jewellery,' Jubilee said, observing his reaction. He didn't seem overly surprised. She unzipped her bag and removed a folder containing her research. Sir Rupert gestured for them to sit at a large round oak table. Jubilee showed him the photos and asked if he possessed any historical documents pertaining to the stolen items.

Meg watched Sir Rupert as Jubilee showed him the police reports and photos of the ruby set made by Starr and Everett. The sight of the Flame of India caused Sir Rupert's eyes to widen in recognition, though he quickly recovered. Meg felt instantly uneasy. It seemed to her that he wasn't pleased the jewellery had been found.

'You actually have these?' he asked.

'Yes,' Jubilee replied. 'Do you have the original receipts?'

'Of course. They would be here somewhere.'

'We're heading to Cornwall tonight,' Meg said. 'If you need time to find them, you can contact us on these mobile numbers or through our email address.' Meg handed Sir Rupert a piece of paper with their details on it.

Jubilee asked, 'Do you happen to have a portrait with the ruby set on display, by any chance?'

Sir Rupert hesitated once again. 'No. I'm afraid the ruby set was stolen shortly after they were presented to my mother.'

How convenient, Meg thought. She didn't trust the man, though she couldn't put her finger on why, but she felt as if she had just walked into a spider's web. She decided to probe him about Alex's email.

'Alex Everett, from Starr and Everett mentioned the robbery might have been an inside job. What do you think about that? Could there be any merit in what she claims?' Meg asked.

'Absolutely not,' Sir Rupert retorted, clearly offended by the suggestion.

'It might not have been anyone working at Harrowgate Hall at the time, but if someone knew you had just purchased this magnificent ruby set, they might have seen an opportunity to steal it,' Meg pressed on.

'I don't know anything about that. My father told me long ago about the robbery. The police came and dusted for fingerprints and later returned with mug shots, but my parents couldn't identify anyone.'

'The thieves clearly knew what they were after and where to look. That would suggest they had some inside knowledge,' Jubilee said, a little more diplomatic than her cousin.

'The police report said a housemaid heard one man call out to another, as they made their escape, "Hurry up, Mallard!". Could you find out if someone named Mallard ever worked here around that time?' Meg asked.

Sir Rupert thought for a moment. 'I'll look into it. But the answer will be no. This house had nothing to do with those robberies. Is that clear?'

'We're not accusing anyone, Sir Rupert, we're just trying to uncover the facts,' Jubilee sensed she had hit a nerve but wasn't sure how far to push him.

'I believe there were some rumours after the robbery, but they were directed towards the jeweller who made the ruby set. But they were only rumours and not substantiated by the police.'

'I see,' Jubilee replied.

Meg exchanged a glance at Jubilee, as if to say, *let's get out of here*. Sir Rupert wasn't forthcoming about anything else. For someone about to come into a sizable fortune he was keen to be rid of them.

After standing up, Sir Rupert finally ventured one final question.

'Have you notified the police yet?'

'Yes, of course. We keep the Australian police updated with our progress. They're liaising with Scotland Yard. Why?' Jubilee asked.

'Just making sure you're being thorough. I'll see what I can discover from our records.'

'We'd appreciate that,' Jubilee said.

'Was the stolen jewellery insured?' Meg asked.

After a brief pause, Sir Rupert replied, 'That's none of your business.'

With that, he rang the bell for the butler to return and escort his guests from the hall.

Jubilee and Meg said their goodbyes at the door of the library and the butler escorted them to the front entrance.

Once they were back in the campervan, Meg remarked, 'Well, he was very quick to get rid of us.'

'I know. Did you get the feeling he was hiding something?'

'Yep. I bet those rubies weren't insured. Even if the other jewellery was, the loss of the rubies would have hurt financially.'

'Did you notice how he was adamant his family had nothing to do with the robberies – plural?'

'Yeah, and in doing so, directed the blame at Starr and Everett. Alex never mentioned it was her firm that was accused of stealing them.'

'No … she didn't. But I've just realised. If someone received an insurance payout, who actually owns the jewellery now? Is it the insurance company?'

'Yep. I've looked into it. If any items are recovered, they would belong to the insurance company. But if they are personal and valuable, the insurer would ask if the owner wanted to keep them. If the owner said yes, the insurer sells the item back to them for the price of the original settlement payout.'

Jubilee looked worried. 'We should have checked first. What if Maryann's jewellery was insured, do you think they could afford to buy it back?'

'Don't panic. The thefts occurred over eighty years ago. Some insurance companies might not exist anymore. Besides, the jewellery is worth far more today than it was back then. Today's sale price would be higher than any previous settlement payout.'

Jubilee felt relieved. She had only just enriched the Hardwicks' and Maryann and Renee's lives, she didn't want to see it all slip away.

'I've just realised, His Lordship never asked if we brought the rubies with us,' Meg pointed out.

'No, he didn't, and he's a sir, not a lord, Meg. Let's keep things in perspective.'

'Yes ma'am,' Meg laughed. 'It's been a long day. How about we head to Cornwall now? Henry said he's looking forward to seeing us and I'm looking forward to a hot bath.'

'Alright,' Jubilee sighed. 'I'll call him and let him know we're on our way.'

*   *   *

'We might have a problem, Giles.'

'What now?'

'Those two Australian women just visited me. They have the Flame of India, and it's been buried in their fucking garden in

some small town called Bowral in Australia all this time. They
think I'm the rightful owner and want documented proof.'

'I doubt Starr and Everett would agree with them,' replied
Giles, flatly.

'What if they know more than they're letting on?'

'How could they?'

'I don't know, Giles. What if they uncovered more than
they're letting on? I won't have my family's name dragged
through the mud. If that happens, yours will too. Fix it.'

Sir Rupert Henley-Smith hung up on his old adversary,
Giles Grimshaw. He walked to the window and watched the
campervan as it made its way down the long driveway.

He cursed his family's ill-fated alliance with the Grimshaws.
Sir Rupert feared the past had finally caught up with his family.
Someone will talk. They always do. He had always dreaded the
day those rubies would resurface and along with them, the
truth about the robbery.

*   *   *

Jubilee's spirits rose once she'd finished talking to Henry
Hawthorn. He was looking forward to meeting them. Henry
had insisted they stay at the hotel instead of their campervan.
Both women were looking forward to a long hot bath and a
large comfortable bed that evening.

Jubilee put St Ives, Cornwall into the map app on her
phone. The drive would take a little over two hours and
forty-five minutes, first on the M5 and then on the A30.
They would arrive after dark, but they were relieved they
wouldn't have to find another campervan site. It had been a
long and tiring day.

As Meg drove, Jubilee kept rehearsing in her head what
she was going to say to Henry when they met. With each

passing mile, she grew more anxious the closer they got to St Ives. A murder had brought them together, but why would Henry hate her for her great-grandfather's actions? Didn't he want answers too?

They drove up the flower-lined driveway of the Hawthorn Hotel just before dusk. The beautiful hotel glowed under floodlights. The large, three-storey mansion was perched high on top of a hill, surrounded by gardens that cascaded down in tiers around the entire estate. They knew the sea was a short walk away, the salty air teasing their senses. They looked forward to seeing the views in the morning, From the second and third levels it would be breathtaking.

After finding directions to a small car park around the side of the hotel, they each packed a small bag and made their way into the hotel.

The entrance opened up to an expansive foyer. The reception desk was to their right, and at the far end was a large fireplace, which was surrounded by comfortable sofas and coffee tables. The opulence of the room was made even more grandiose by the large portraits and landscapes that adored the walls around them. One hallway led guests to a dining room, while another opened up to a bar and lounge. They also saw signs directing them to a library and a day spa.

'Hello, can I help you?' asked the receptionist.

'Yes. We're here to see Henry Hawthorn. He's expecting us. My name is Jubilee Jones, and this is Meg Forrester.'

'Please take a seat over there,' she said, indicating to the chairs near the fireplace. 'I'll let him know you've arrived.'

Meg flopped herself down on the sofa and made herself comfortable. They felt relaxed and welcomed as they took in the foyer's ambience. Unlike Harrowgate Hall earlier that day, this place radiated warmth and charm.

While Meg was talking about soaking in a bubble bath, Jubilee noticed a young man walking briskly toward the receptionist. He was in his mid-thirties, slim, and dressed in a polo shirt and jeans. His wavy dark hair touched his shoulders. He walked with an air of confidence, like someone who knew where they belonged. He spoke to the receptionist, who nodded towards Jubilee and Meg. Whether it was nerves at finally meeting him, or because she thought he was one of the most handsome men she'd ever met, Jubilee's heart skipped a beat.

Turning towards them, Henry gave Jubilee a wide grin, which stretched from ear to ear. Then he walked over to them. Jubilee quickly stood up, self-consciously brushing her fingers through her hair.

'Hello, you must be Jubilee and Meg,' he said, extending his hand.

'Yes. I'm Jubilee, and this is my cousin, Meg.'

'It's a pleasure to finally meet you both. I'm Henry Hawthorn.'

Meg stood up and approached Henry, shaking his hand. If she didn't know Jubilee any better, she would have said she was blushing.

'I have so many questions to ask you about my ancestor, Jack Hawthorn. But it's getting late. I have a lovely room ready for you. I was hoping you would join me for dinner tonight. It's been hectic here all day. There's always something breaking in a house this old. I'll understand if you're tired and would like to leave it until tomorrow.'

'We'd love to,' Jubilee replied, putting an end to Meg's bubble bath.

'Smashing! Let's say 7:30 in the dining room.'

Henry fetched Jubilee and Meg's room key and escorted them to their room.

'Susan insisted on joining us. I told her all about you. I think she's worried that you might be trying to scam something out of us. She thinks I'm a softie.'

Both women were surprised but smiled at Henry all the same. They couldn't really blame her.

'We get that a lot,' Meg said, as they climbed up the grand staircase.

'We're looking forward to meeting your wife,' Jubilee said, sounding a little discouraged.

'What! Oh gosh, Susan's not my wife, good lord, she's my sister,' he said, grinning at them. Jubilee quickly looked away, trying to stifle a smile.

When they reached their room, Henry held the door open for them. He gave them a slight nod before taking his leave.

Once inside their room, Meg said, 'I'm starving. But I'm going to find their library before heading into the dining room.'

'You and your bloody books.'

'Everyone needs a passion. My literary love affairs take me all over the world and through many centuries whenever I choose to travel on any given evening. And if I'm not wholly satisfied with my dalliances, I simply close that chapter of my life and open another one.'

Jubilee laughed at her cousin's analogy. She envied her simplistic passion.

*   *   *

Jubilee and Meg entered the dining room at quarter to eight, with Jubilee having to pull Meg out of the library. They spotted Henry at a table with a young woman with short-cropped red hair. Henry introduced his sister, Susan. After the introductions, they ordered their meal, while Henry offered to choose the wine from their cellar.

'My brother told me about your investigation into Jack Hawthorn's death. That you might know who killed him.'

'It's a lot more complicated than that,' Meg replied.

Hopefully, for a final time, Jubilee recounted her story. This time it included the bodies discovered in the Plymouth sewer. Jubilee handed over Jack Hawthorn's passport from her handbag and gave it to Henry, along with the photo she'd found inside.

Henry and Susan examined it closely for some time.

'Oh my god,' exclaimed Susan. 'We have the exact same picture in our living room. All this time, it was buried in your garden.'

'I'm sorry,' Jubilee said again.

'It's not your fault. Why ever would you think that?' Henry said, matter-of-factly. Jubilee could only smile as Henry put her at ease. She felt no anxiousness beside him.

'We think our great-grandfather killed Jack and took his identity to escape England. We believe Jack Hawthorn was simply in the wrong place at the wrong time,' Meg explained.

Jubilee asked Henry if he had come across any further correspondence or diary entries that would clarify what happened during the police investigation.

'I've found some letters from Jack's mother to the police, both before and after they discovered Jack's body,' he said. 'She hired a private investigator, but he only managed to find one witness who said she saw a young man fitting Jack Hawthorn's description in a fight down an alley. But she couldn't even remember the exact night. She said there were three men involved. One was older, medium to slim build, with light brown hair, and the other was a very tall, broad-shouldered man, with dark orangey red hair. The note mentioned she didn't hang around because she didn't want to get involved. She thought it was just another drunken street brawl.'

Jubilee scratched her head, looking a bit confused.

'Our great-grandfather was average build with light brown hair,' she said, unconvinced. 'But that could be describing anyone.'

'The private investigator offered a reward. Maybe she told him some tale just for the money,' Susan said.

'The police believed there might have been three robbers involved. He could be the third one,' Meg said.

Henry was eager to help. 'We can go through all the documents tomorrow. Hopefully, there'll be no more emergencies to deal with.'

When their meals arrived, the mood lightened when they shifted their conversation to their lives in Australia and what they had gotten up to since arriving. Not wanting to put a dampener on the night, Jubilee hoped they wouldn't ask her if she enjoyed her meal. She had been a little disappointed in it. Her fish was too dry and the salmoriglio sauce did nothing to add to its flavour. Although, it was the only negative thing she could say about the hotel. She knew a great restaurant could make or break a hotel like this.

'You have a beautiful home here. When did you decide to turn it into a hotel?' she asked.

'About ten years ago. My sister and I inherited it from our parents.'

'Oh, I'm sorry to hear that,' Jubilee said.

'No, no. They're not dead,' he said. 'My parents bought a house on the Italian Riviera. When my father's health took a bad turn, they decided to spend half the year, the colder part that is, in a warmer climate. They handed the house to Susan and me, and with their blessing, we transformed it into a hotel. These houses cost a fortune to run. It's money down the gurgler unless you have plenty of income to keep them up. Unfortunately, we don't earn anything from the estate, so we decided to pool our resources together and turn it into a hotel.'

'How exciting!' Jubilee said.

'It will be if we can make a go of it. The bank lent us the money because we had a sound business plan, and we both sold our apartments. We have a beautiful hotel in a perfect location. Everything was going smoothly for a few years until COVID struck. We had to let most of our staff go. However, when we finally re-opened a lot of our original staff were no longer available. Our sous chef is running the kitchen until we can find a new head chef. He's done a good job but he hates it. He's not qualified and it's stressing him out.'

That explained a lot, Jubilee thought, smiling to herself.

'Jubilee knows that all too well. She was the head chef at one of Sydney's finest restaurants but lost her job because of the pandemic. Now, she's thinking of opening her own restaurant.'

Jubilee shot Meg a look.

'Really?' Henry said. 'Any help you can give us, we're all ears.'

'Henry, she didn't come all this way to cook in our restaurant,' Susan interjected.

'Sorry,' he said, getting ahead of himself.

'It's fine. I don't mind,' Jubilee smiled. 'I'll be happy to advise you in any way I can. It's the least I can do for putting us up.'

'Thank you,' Susan said, glancing at her brother. 'But honestly, what did you think of your meals tonight?'

'Lovely,' Meg said, smiling diplomatically. But Jubilee couldn't sugar-coat her opinion, not when it came to food.

'Well,' Jubilee said, 'my fish was overcooked and the salmoriglio sauce wasn't rich enough. It's supposed to complement the fish, unfortunately, it fell short.'

'I'm sorry. We're in dire need of a head chef. This is a five-star hotel, our restaurant deserves a five-star chef,' Susan explained.

'Don't apologise,' Jubilee protested. 'Many restaurants have struggled in Australia, as I'm sure they have here. But you're right, you do need a highly qualified chef, a Michelin-starred chef if you can find one. But they won't come cheap.'

Meg saw an opportunity to pitch an idea. 'Well, while we're here, why don't you help them out in the kitchen, Jubes? She's a cracker of a chef, and I know she's eager to get back into a kitchen.'

Jubilee glared at Meg once again to no avail. 'I wouldn't want to impose.'

'Poppycock,' Henry interjected, banging his hand on the table. 'Michael, our sous chef, would be thrilled to have your help.'

'That settles it then,' Meg said, mischievously. 'If your offer to stay here still stands, while we wait to hear back from Grimshaw Manor and Harrowgate Hall, Jubilee can help out with your chef problem, and I'll keep investigating the last two estates.'

'That's fine by me,' Susan agreed.

Although Jubilee felt her decision had been made for her, she was secretly excited to get back into a professional kitchen again.

The remainder of the evening rolled by too quickly for Jubilee, who enjoyed Henry and Susan's company immensely. She genuinely felt a pang of sadness when it was time to say goodnight.

It was well past twelve when Jubilee and Meg finally made it back to their room.

'I guess I'll have my bath tomorrow,' Meg said, feeling too tired to contemplate one now. 'Earth to Jubilee.'

'What?'

'If I didn't know any better, I'd say you like him.'

'Don't be silly. I've only just met him,' Jubilee replied, grabbing her pyjamas and heading to the bathroom.

'True, but it feels like you've been searching for him your whole life,' Meg muttered to herself, as she climbed into bed. She knew her cousin all too well and hadn't seen her so jubilant and expressive in a long time.

As Meg lay awake, she thought of conspiring ways in which to help encourage her cousin with this impasse until she figured it out for herself. She would have to play matchmaker, like Jane Austen's *Emma*.

Chapter Twenty Two

St Ives

July 14 – Friday morning – Day 10

Meg let out a contented sigh as she soaked in her bubble bath. *Heaven*, she thought as she picked up her book and flicked to the last place she had read. Jubilee was already downstairs exploring the kitchen and assisting with the breakfast service.

In the kitchen, Henry introduced Jubilee to Michael, the sous chef. The breakfast menu was straightforward, like most hotels, so Jubilee offered to help make the poached eggs and omelettes. By the time Meg came down for breakfast at nine, Jubilee had already been in the kitchen for over three hours. When Jubilee finally walked into the dining room, Meg immediately noticed the change in her cousin.

'You miss it, don't you?'

'Yes, I do,' Jubilee replied, smiling. 'It's hectic but exhilarating. I miss the adrenalin. I told Michael I would help him with the dinner menu. Spice it up a bit. Plus, there's room for a few daily specials. He's just been so swamped with the regular menu that he hasn't had time to get creative.'

'Knock yourself out, Jubes! I'm going to spend the morning sightseeing, then I'll contact Ms Up Herself again. Hopefully, our charming housekeeper will be more forthcoming this time. I know she's hiding something.'

'Why don't we go to the beach together? I'll speak with Michael after lunch since I want to check out their fish market.'

'Sounds like a plan. You know, I've always liked your poached eggs,' Meg said with a smile, as she finished off her breakfast.

They caught up with Henry in the foyer, who was eager to show them his favourite spots around St Ives. Time was fleeting for Jubilee while in his company, but Meg felt like a third wheel. Henry was obviously enchanted with her cousin. When they arrived back at the hotel after 2:00 pm, Meg decided to take her leave.

'On that note, I'll crack on with why we're actually here,' Meg said.

'Thanks,' Jubilee said. 'I'll be in the kitchen if you need anything.'

'How about we meet tonight at my apartment?' Henry said. 'It's where Susan and I live in a little ground-floor apartment. The receptionist can point you in the right direction. Let's say after dinner, at about ten?'

'Great!' Jubilee replied.

'See you then,' Meg said as she headed back to their room.

Henry led Jubilee to the kitchen, and over a quick cup of coffee, Jubilee spoke more about her restaurant in Sydney.

'We changed our menu each season and always used the freshest local products in season. We also got creative with our weekly specials,' she said, remembering her time at The Mariner. 'It's important to do that, if you want regulars to keep coming back. Some people love their favourites, but others want variety and you need to cater for both if you want them to return. I'll make you two of my signature dishes. A spicy Mediterranean lamb dish and a delicious seafood dish that I was experimenting with before we closed. I'll use your local fish, which is always important. I checked earlier, and you have the ingredients I need. If you like them, you can add them as specials tonight.'

'That sounds awesome,' Henry replied. 'I need to leave you now as I have to check on the maintenance crew and see if yesterday's problem has been fixed before today's occurs.'

Jubilee chuckled at Henry's laid-back offhanded manner to his hotel's afflictions.

*   *   *

In her room, Meg opened up Jubilee's new computer and began sifting through her emails and contacts on ancestry.dot.com. She hadn't bothered to replace her old one, as she had her iPad with her, and her work computer back home.

Meg left another voicemail for Ms Upton asking if there was any news from Lord and Lady Grimshaw. There wasn't, so Meg gave Ms Upton her current address at St Ives. She felt a little thrill when she noticed another email from Billy.

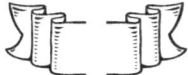

Dear Meg,

Thank you for Maryann Bishop's details. I have forwarded them to the British police for further investigation.

I've not found anything new regarding the robbery at Harrowgate Hall. The police mentioned there were insinuations of an inside job, directed at a jeweller, but there was no proof to suggest they were involved. They interviewed both partners, Winston Starr and Felix Everett at the time, but they denied any involvement. Unfortunately, as the saying goes, 'mud sticks', and their reputations took a hit.

We've also received more documentation from James Hawkins at Bromley House at Cheltenham and Jonathan Hardwick has been in contact. He's located the wills for Thomas and Sofia Hardwick and will send them over soon. I know it feels like a long process, but the Australian Police will need to verify the ownership before they approve the transfer of stolen goods back to England. After that, Scotland Yard can take over.

I've organised for a police car to drive by your house at least three times a day to ensure everything is alright.

Can't wait to catch up in person next week.

Warm regards

Billy

How sweet, Meg thought. She was tempted to call him, but the time difference held her back, so she opted to send him an email instead. She plugged her mobile phone into the laptop to charge it, then searched online for more information about the Grimshaws and Henley-Smiths. Grabbing a small bottle of wine from the minibar, she settled on the couch in her room to view her findings.

Whether it was the wine or the excessive amount of walking she'd done since arriving in England, Meg started to feel drowsy. Her eyes kept drooping. Usually, she spent her days sitting behind the counter of her bookshop or snuggled up with a good book. She hadn't realised how unfit she was. She promised herself she would remedy that once she returned home, but then again, as they say, *if wishes were horses*. For now, she was happy to relax with her wine and a chocolate bar.

While browsing, she stumbled upon an old website featuring Lord and Lady Grimshaw at a children's charity event. The website showcased photos of the guests and the items up for auction. The event was over two years ago, but what caught Meg's attention was the jewellery that Lady Joanna was wearing. Ignoring the couture evening gown, Meg was drawn to her earrings. Their design looked strikingly similar to the emerald earrings that were missing from Bromley House, the first house robbed in 1939. She recognised the design, as it was quite distinctive.

Meg quickly got up from the couch and searched through Jubilee's folder to find the printouts of their design. There was no doubt about it. Meg was convinced they were part of the emerald set stolen from Bromley House.

'What the hell?' she exclaimed, no longer feeling drowsy. 'That can't be!'

Meg double-checked the police report from the Bromley House robbery. The report had a few black and white photographs of some stolen items, which Thomas Hardwick had kept for insurance purposes. It was the hand-drawn design from Lieberman and Bach that showed the design and colour.

Meg sat down at the table and wondered what the hell was going on. She thought of calling Lieberman and Bach, but it was Alex Everett who first insinuated the idea of an inside job. Meg was sure Alex was hiding something, and besides, her time in England was slipping away. They desperately needed answers. Meg dialled Alex's number and this time she was put straight through.

'Hello, Meg. How can I help you?'

'I need a favour. Can you help me verify a pair of earrings that were stolen from the Hawkins estate in 1939?' Meg asked.

'Send over the details and I'll see what I can do. Did we design them for the Hawkins family?'

'No. They were designed by Lieberman and Bach. But they weren't in Jubilee's biscuit tin. I've just seen Lady Joanna Grimshaw wearing them at a charity event two years ago.'

The line was silent for five long seconds.

'Are you still there, Alex?'

'Yes, I'm here. We need to meet. I can't discuss this over the phone. Where are you?'

'I'm at the Hawthorn Hotel at St Ives, Cornwall.'

'I'll be there tonight. Don't mention this to anyone.'

'Why not?' Meg asked, thinking Alex was being a tad melodramatic.

'Your great-grandfather may have committed those robberies, but I always thought Harrowgate Hall was involved. Now, I'm not so sure. I'll explain everything when I arrive. But one thing you need to know. The Flame of India belongs to my family.'

'The rubies?'

'Yes. The necklace, earrings, ring, and bracelet. The entire set belongs to Starr and Everett, not the Henley-Smiths.'

Alex ended the call. Meg poured herself another glass of wine.

Sometime later, Meg headed into the bathroom to freshen up. It was nearly 7:00 pm, giving her an hour to search for more photos of the Grimshaws. She was meeting Jubilee for dinner at 8:00 pm, followed by drinks with Henry and Susan. *One more guest can't hurt*, Meg thought. It was going to be an interesting night.

Meg headed downstairs early and thought a quick walk in the gardens would be nice before dinner. The evening air was refreshing, with the salty sea breeze and the sound of the seagulls overhead. The grounds were pleasant and complemented the hotel's charm. Meg could see why the hotel was popular for weddings. She wished her mother was here to appreciate their design.

Arriving at dinner, Meg updated Jubilee on the mystery of the emerald earrings and Alex's strange phone call.

'How the hell did Lady Grimshaw end up with the Hardwick's earrings?' Jubilee asked, clearly puzzled. She began twirling her ring around and around on her finger, her anxiety growing with the unexpected events.

'Hopefully, we'll get some answers when Alex shows up.'

Jubilee and Meg enjoyed a nice dinner together. She chose the special that Jubilee had just added to the menu, and it seemed like a lot of the other guests did too.

When they arrived at Henry and Susan's apartment, they were warmly welcomed and offered a drink. Meg told Henry and Susan about her latest online discovery and recounted her conversation with Alex.

Susan was amazed when Meg showed her the website. Henry, on the other hand, was still sceptical about this new turn of events and how it could be related to the death of his great-uncle.

Jubilee could only shake her head, feeling a bit lost. She didn't have an answer for him. Their investigation had taken a surprising turn, leaving everyone a bit bamboozled about what to do next.

'Looks like there may be five of us tonight for drinks. Alex seemed a bit eager to get here. Hopefully, she'll have more answers for us,' Meg said.

Henry changed the subject. 'Thanks Jubilee, for your help today. Michael had nothing but praise about you. How long do you plan to stay in England?'

'Ah, less than a week, I'm afraid. Meg needs to get back to her bookshop, and I have to finish redecorating my house and find a new job. Hopefully, we'll have spoken to everyone involved by then.'

'Oh,' Henry seemed disappointed.

'But you know,' Meg interrupted, 'she's kind of unemployed back home, so there's really no rush for her to get back if she was offered another job?' Meg was unapologetic about putting her cousin on the spot with Henry and Susan.

Jubilee felt her cheeks flush red. She glared at Meg. But the idea wasn't completely far-fetched. She only had her part-time job at the bakery waiting for her. Not that she'd miss it.

Meg handed Henry and Susan the documentation they received from the National Archives and their own research. Henry did the same with his grandmother's journal and private documents. Together, they compared notes and once they had reviewed all the paperwork, Jubilee remembered the scarf she'd brought along. She pulled it out of her bag and gave it to Henry and Susan.

'I guess this belongs to you. I found it in my attic.' She showed them the label hand-stitched into it: *J.H. With Love, M.H.* Susan read the inscription then gently rubbed her hand over the scarf, feeling a bit surreal about the whole thing. The moment was interrupted by the ringing of a telephone. Henry jumped up to answer it.

The receptionist told him that Alex Everett was at the front desk to see Meg Forrester.

'I'll come out and fetch her,' Henry said. Turning back to everyone, he said, 'back in a jiffy.'

Before long, Henry returned to the apartment, and right behind him was Alex Everett. After everyone was introduced, Alex was given a drink before she explained why her visit was so urgent.

Taking out a folder from her bag, she opened it to show them all some old documents.

'I'm only interested in the ruby set you showed me. The large ruby in the centre of the necklace is called the Flame of India. It's very rare and one of the largest rubies in existence. The rubies in the bracelet, earrings, and ring are also of the highest quality. It's hard to estimate the value of the rubies in today's market, but a conservative estimate would value this set at around ten million US dollars. Possibly, a lot higher.'

'Holy shit!' Meg exclaimed, spilling some of her drink into her lap as she sat up straight in her chair.

Jubilee questioned Alex, 'You told us the other day it was worth only two million?'

'I did. I didn't want to reveal too much until I was sure you were genuine.'

'Why do you believe they belong to you?' Jubilee pressed.

'The jewellery set was made for Sir Malcolm Henley-Smith, to give to his wife for her birthday shortly after they were married. Only, it turns out he couldn't afford them. The jewellery was delivered in good faith, but a few days later the bank rejected his cheque. Once my grandfather realised the oversight he contacted Sir Malcolm, who apologised profusely and assured him it would rectified. Only he never did. A few days later, the Flame of India had been stolen. Too convenient for my liking, and unfortunately, Sir Malcolm hadn't insured them. Why would he if he couldn't afford to buy it? Which means, legally, the ruby set belongs to Starr and Everett.'

'Jesus, and you think he staged his own robbery?' Henry asked.

'Yes, my grandfather did, and so did I, but now …?'

'But the Henley-Smiths accused him,' Jubilee said. 'Why didn't he inform the police that the jewels weren't paid for by the Henley-Smiths at the time?'

'Because, in their eyes, it would've given him a motive to steal them back,' Alex replied. 'The police couldn't prove my grandfather had anything to do with the robbery, but he couldn't prove that he didn't. The accusations destroyed him, physically and emotionally. His reputation meant everything to him. Then when you mentioned that you saw Lady Grimshaw wearing the emerald earrings at the charity event, I now have to believe that the Grimshaw family was involved in the robbery somehow. I'm not sure what to think anymore.'

'How do we prove it was them?' Henry asked.

'Jubilee, Meg,' Alex said. 'I believe your great-grandfather did commit these robberies. At least the first four and he would have had a fence to sell the jewellery to. What I think happened was they got caught at Grimshaw Manor in Bath. Maybe the Grimshaw family saw an opportunity to steal the rubies from the Henley-Smiths. You see, the Grimshaws attended a birthday party at Harrowgate Hall on the night Sir Malcolm gave the ruby set to his wife for her birthday. But, I still can't picture Lord Grimshaw being involved in that robbery, especially that of a friend. Which is why I always thought Sir Malcolm staged his own robbery, then sold off the jewellery and claimed on the insurance for the items insured to lessen his debts. It makes sense now, if Tom Fields was shot before the fifth robbery. Maybe your great-grandfather fled after Tom's death. But that doesn't explain how the rubies came into your great-grandfather's possession.'

'Do you know the exact date when Tom Fields was shot?' Henry asked. 'He was found along a roadside, but he could have been killed anywhere and just left there. Forensics in 1939 was less advanced than today.'

'That's a fair point,' remarked Jubilee, pulling out the police report on Tom Fields's death. 'It only stated the type of gun used, as bullet fragments were found in the body, but it didn't specify the precise time of death.'

Henry continued, 'It's possible he was killed while at Grimshaw Manor. It may also explain why the Grimshaws possess those earrings from the first robbery. Maybe Tom dropped them, or he was caught during the robbery. It could also explain why your great-grandfather had the rubies; the Grimshaws may have persuaded him to steal them, and then agreed to let him go free.'

'Jesus … That's stretching it a little – but doable. How will we ever prove it?' Susan asked, her curiosity growing by the minute.

'I've done my own research over the years, as did my father,' Alex said. 'It turns out, the Henley-Smiths and the Grimshaws faced financial difficulties before the outbreak of World War Two. Like many in their society, they struggled to adapt to the modern world, and didn't know how to survive in it. They needed to marry off their sons and daughters well. The Grimshaws had sold a large portion of their estate in 1935. However, after the war, they appeared to be financially well-off again.'

Jubilee asked, 'So you now think the Grimshaws were involved because they have the emerald earrings?'

'Yes,' Alex replied. 'I initially thought the Henley-Smiths conspired to commit fraud by claiming they were robbed too. But, since you had the rubies all along, they *were* actually robbed. Now my theories have all gone up in smoke. All I know for sure is that the Grimshaws were involved somehow, and the Flame of India belongs to my family.'

Alex shared what happened to her family and their business after the robberies in 1939.

'The theft nearly destroyed my grandfather. However, it was later towards the end of the war, that he learned the fate of so many Jews in Europe, including members of his own family that he suffered a heart attack, and died.'

'I'm sorry, Alex, to hear what happened to your grandfather,' Jubilee said, feeling that familiar wave of regret again.

'Thank you, but my grandfather's partner, Winston Starr, also suffered. He was a co-founder and his family lost a great deal during that time too. The rubies were insured of course, but once the insurer got wind that my family was accused of being a part of their theft, they refused to pay until their investigation was complete. Then the war began, and the insurance company went under by the time it ended.'

'I'm sorry,' Meg said.

'Winston's son was killed in the war, and after Winston himself died in 1969, his wife and children left London. They're a silent partner now, but it took thirty years of hard work to rebuild the company. My family had no involvement in any robbery. It would be unthinkable. We create works of art, we don't destroy them.'

'I can imagine that after the war there were black markets flush with stolen jewellery and heirlooms stolen by the Nazis. It couldn't have been difficult to shift stolen jewellery during that time,' Susan remarked.

'That's what my family believed. The rubies were lost long ago. But when you walked into my office last week, it reignited that fire in me to uncover the truth.'

'If you can prove the Henley-Smiths never paid for the ruby set, then they rightfully belong to you,' Jubilee said.

'Thank you. We still have the bank cheque and the letter from the bank confirming the cheque bounced and was never replaced.'

'But I'm a little confused,' Meg said. 'I can understand how the Grimshaws caught them in the act and killed Tom Fields. But that doesn't explain how Jack Jones still had the jewellery from the first three robberies.'

Alex shrugged, 'Maybe he stashed the jewellery somewhere before each robbery … I don't know. Now, thanks to you, I can prove the Grimshaws were involved somehow.'

Everyone was silent for a moment, until Susan spoke up.

'Our family has waited over eighty years to uncover the truth about Jack Hawthorn, Alex, and yet we may never know who killed him. I'm happy for you, but there has to be a connection between these robberies and Jack Hawthorn.'

Jubilee ran her hands through her hair, feeling frustrated. There could be countless possibilities.

Meg broke the silence.

'Someone broke into Jubes's house back in Bowral and into our campervan a few days ago searching for something,' she said. 'Maybe someone suspects we know more about the robberies than we're letting on, which could potentially incriminate someone somehow. Or, they think we know where the rest of the stolen jewellery is hidden.'

'Oh my god! Do you believe it's someone connected to either the Grimshaw or Henley-Smith families?' Henry asked.

'Now I do,' Meg replied.

'Then strike while the iron is hot,' Susan advised. 'Spread the word and see if anyone bites. You have all the proof you need, if someone is after something they'll think twice about coming after you again if the media gets involved.'

'That could be risky,' Henry replied, sounding concerned. 'I don't want either of you to get hurt.'

'But it might trigger a response,' Jubilee said, blushing at his concern.

'What if Jubilee and Meg announce their discovery?' Alex asked. 'It would make a great news story. The value of the jewellery alone would catch people's attention. Then, they could hint at fraud and murder.'

'That's not a bad idea,' Susan agreed. 'The tabloids love a scandal, especially when it involves the well-to-do.'

Jubilee expressed concern, stating, 'How can we prove those earrings are in fact the ones stolen from Bromley House? If they aren't, the Grimshaw family could sue us for slander.'

'Maybe we should let the police handle the Grimshaws,' Meg suggested. 'If those earrings came from Bromley House, then it's definitely a job for the police. I'll ask Billy to contact Scotland Yard, and they can take it from there. The Grimshaws will need to provide proof of ownership. If they can't, the police will check the engravings and determine who made them and for whom.'

Everyone agreed it was a good plan. It was time to get the police directly involved.

Alex called her sister, Rose to get the ball rolling. She asked her to contact their PR company to organise some media coverage. Rose had some ideas to get the story spreading on social media, too.

'Well Jubes, this will be our fifteen minutes of fame,' Meg said. 'We better wash our hair tomorrow.'

'Don't joke. This is all happening very fast.' Jubilee's private but determined quest was about to get national coverage and notoriety. She hadn't expected it to escalate so fast. She was growing more anxious by the minute.

'If you don't want to talk to the police, I'll do it myself,' Meg said, noticing her cousin's strained expression.

'No. We'll face it together. I started this so I need to see it through, no matter what happens.'

'You're both safe here. I'll protect you,' Henry assured them. His remark made Susan giggle.

'What?' he exclaimed.

'You were screaming a month ago when a baby squirrel ran over your foot. I had to capture it and put it outside. Remember?'

'That's different. They've always scared me.'

'Don't worry ladies. Your room locks are secure and we have the best security system money can buy. No one can enter the hotel without being detected and we have a direct line to the police in case of emergencies.'

Jubilee was touched. 'Thanks, Susan, and you too, Henry. We appreciate you letting us stay here.'

'I should be the one thanking you,' he replied. 'We've received a number of compliments about our dinner menu tonight. Several locals promised to return next week.'

'It was nothing, really. I love creating new and exciting dishes. I should thank you, I enjoyed myself tonight.'

Alex stifled another yawn and politely bid her goodnight. She had booked a room at the hotel and would stay as long as she was needed. Her departure prompted Susan and Meg to say their goodnights as well, leaving Henry and Jubilee alone.

Jubilee wasn't tired in the least, but didn't want to outstay her welcome.

'I better go too, Henry. You must be tired.'

'No. Not unless you are.'

'Not at all. I thought we could talk more about the menu, I have a few more ideas I'd like to run past you. If you agree, I'll speak to Michael in the morning, after breakfast. We can create a few more dishes for you and Susan to try. I can help design your menus around the seasons so you can highlight all the local ingredients. I noticed the hotel has an amazing vegetable garden and greenhouse. You should definitely take advantage of it. It's looking a bit wild and unkempt.'

'I couldn't agree more. Our head chef had a similar idea. Unfortunately, he returned to France, so it's been neglected ever since.'

'Good, that's settled then. I'll help you design a five-star menu befitting your magnificent hotel.'

'I'm glad you like it.'

'What's not to like, Henry? It's warm and inviting, you're in a perfect location, especially for weddings and events. You should consider offering a morning tea or high tea, which, in good weather, you could host outside on the terrace and around the gardens in summer. It will surely be a great success.'

Henry was captivated by Jubilee's enthusiasm and passion. She was easy to talk to; very attractive, and incredibly charming, making it hard for him to concentrate as he was drawn by her warmth and smile.

As they talked, their conversation drifted towards their personal lives. Jubilee found herself opening up about her life in Sydney. She explained how The Mariner had been a successful restaurant, but she had felt adrift and alone in the beautiful city and often wondered what was missing in her life. Jubilee had thought returning home would help her find what she was looking for. But it hadn't.

Henry could relate to Jubilee's feelings of disconnection. He had studied economics at university, but after working for ten years in London, his passion for finance diminished and he found himself soul-searching about his future and life. Transforming his family home into a hotel was the best decision he had ever made. He had no regrets about investing everything he had into the hotel, though the last few years had been difficult.

Their conversation was interrupted when Jubilee heard the clock chime the hour. It was 1:00 am. She was sad to say goodnight. Henry walked her to the door, and before she left, he softly kissed her on the cheek and said goodnight. As Jubilee walked through the quiet hotel lobby and ascended the steps, one at a time to the first floor, she felt a wave a happiness wash over her. How could one simple kiss leave her in such a euphoric state?

As she entered their room, Jubilee had thought Meg would be asleep, but instead she found her still awake, on Jubilee's computer.

Meg glanced up at her cousin, who was still in a state of exuberance, as she ambled into the room. Meg couldn't help but smile.

Jubilee stared back, but all she could only was, 'What?'

It wasn't until 1:30 am that Meg closed the laptop and they both turned off their bedside lamps. Jubilee watched the moon shining outside her window, illuminating the room. She didn't bother to close the curtains. Instead, she lay awake watching the moon until sleep eventually took her for the night. With a smile on her face, she drifted off in a peaceful slumber.

Chapter Twenty Three

Hawthorn Hotel, St Ives

July 15 – Saturday mid-morning – Day 11

In the kitchen, Jubilee was preparing her signature dishes with Michael to present to Henry and Susan, in the hope they would be added to the evening's menu.

Alex found Meg in the garden enjoying a club sandwich for a late breakfast. They had both been busy on their phones all morning. Alex had picked up some juicy gossip along the Hatton Garden grapevine.

'I was told I would find you here,' she said, as she sat down next to Meg.

'I'm just taking a quick break. How about you?' Meg replied.

'Me too. I have some more gossip for you. I've been informed that in the early 1930s, Lord Grimshaw was a partner in a diamond mine in South Africa, with his brother-in-law and a jewellery company no longer active. The mine was unsuccessful and collapsed, which could explain why he had to sell parts of his estate over the years. He may have fallen into debt, which might explain his involvement in the robbery and insurance fraud.'

'Could he have used the mine as a cover, to sell off at least the diamonds and claim they were from his own mine?'

'That's a possibility, but he would need a broker or jeweller willing to buy them. Besides, if the mine was worthless, the jewellery trade would have been aware of that. I'll ask Peter Lockwood to investigate the partnership further. If that family owned, or partially owned a mine, he'll unearth it.'

'Well done, Alex. I spoke to my mum this morning. She has organised for the bank in Bowral to transfer the jewellery back to England. Billy has liaised with the English police to receive them and handle the transfer.'

'Thank you! This has been a long time coming for my family.'

'The Grimshaws and Henley-Smiths are in for a big surprise when the police come knocking,' Meg giggled.

'Don't underestimate them. If their reputations are at stake, they'll show their claws and fight back.'

* * *

Grimshaw Manor, Bath

'You bloody fool,' yelled Lord Giles Grimshaw. 'What were you thinking, allowing those two women into my house?'

Ms Upton apologised profusely. 'I'm very sorry, sir. They possessed information concerning the robbery in 1939. I thought you would be interested in what they had to say.'

Lord and Lady Grimshaw had returned home earlier that morning. Contrary to what Jubilee and Meg were told, they hadn't been overseas. Instead, they had been staying at their apartment in London for the last week. They returned home as soon as Ms Upton informed them about her unexpected visitors.

'What did they ask you?' Lady Joanna demanded. Her tone was flat but more temperate.

'They wanted to speak to the families of the estates that were robbed by their great-grandfather. They were after information about the robberies. They had police reports and photographs of some of the stolen jewellery.'

'What did you tell them?' Lord Grimshaw said, calming a little. Ms Upton paused before answering.

'Nothing.'

'Keep it that way. If you want to keep your job, keep your mouth shut.'

'Yes, sir.' Ms Upton nodded, understanding the gravity of the situation.

She walked back to her small apartment in the old servant's quarters. Sitting down on the wooden chair, she contemplated her future. A life of service was all she had ever known. This house was her home, for better or worse. As a sense of calm washed over her she knew what she had to do. She bent down, and from under her bed, she pulled out her old suitcase and unlocked it. Ms Upton removed a large envelope from her case and emptied its contents on the bed. She gazed down at the diary that had been entrusted to her mother a lifetime ago, its cover adorned with gold leaf butterflies. Inside the front cover was a hand-written notation.

Diary of Lady Jane Grimshaw, 1939

Ms Upton re-read the note again and fully understood its meaning. *Let justice be done.*

Her mother often talked about loyalty. A housekeeper was always present but rarely seen. That was the lesson her mother had instilled in her many years ago. What was spoken within these walls was kept within these walls. Yet, throughout her time as housekeeper at Grimshaw Manor, Ms Upton had witnessed no loyalty, only greed and selfishness, repeated generation after generation. She sat in silence for a long time, hugging the diary to her chest. She knew her next move would cost her both her job and her home.

With a heavy heart, she wrote a note to Lord Grimshaw, then packed her bag and left Grimshaw Manor through the servant's entrance for the very last time, not daring to look back.

Chapter Twenty Four

July 15 – Saturday afternoon – Day 11

*M*eg returned to her room to continue her research into the Grimshaw family tree.

She logged into her Ancestry account and noticed a new contact for the Grimshaw family. So far, her search for relatives of Tom Fields and Hughie McBean had yielded nothing, which she was silently pleased about. She hadn't needed to go back any further than the early 1900s, but among the names of the Grimshaw descendants, one particular name caught her attention.

Lord Robert and Lady Margaret Grimshaw had three children: Eloise, Robert and Gregory. Robert inherited Grimshaw Manor, while their second son, Gregory, joined the military. Their eldest child, and least likely to inherit the estate was their daughter, Eloise. In 1934, she married Patrick Mallard.

Meg was instantly alert. She ignored her other searches and focused her attention on the Mallard family.

By late afternoon, Meg was convinced Patrick Mallard had to be the second unidentified man found in the Plymouth sewer. Her searches revealed nothing on his whereabouts

203

from 1939. Eloise re-married in 1948, after a magistrate had signed his death certificate, stating he had died in an accident in 1940. The magistrate was none other than Sir Malcolm Henley-Smith II.

The phrase 'as thick as thieves' came to mind as Meg wrote down all the relevant facts she could uncover about Patrick Mallard, from his birth to his education and occupations, which were sketchy, to say the least. He had met Robert Grimshaw while studying at Cambridge, and Meg assumed he was introduced to Eloise through her brother.

Excited about her new discovery, Meg quickly texted everyone and asked them all to join her in the bar. She gathered her evidence and headed downstairs, eager to reveal all to Jubilee, Alex, Henry and Susan.

*   *   *

'I've found him,' Meg shouted, as she burst into the bar, waving a piece of paper in one hand and her iPad in another.

'Who?' Susan asked, looking curious.

'Mallard. I've identified him.'

'Who's Mallard?' Susan asked again.

'He was the other thief from the fifth robbery at Harrowgate Hall. We only knew him as Mallard,' Jubilee explained to Susan and Henry.

'How the hell did you manage that?' Alex asked, clearly impressed.

'Never underestimate the power of free information,' Meg said, grinning from ear to ear.

'Well, don't keep us in suspense,' Jubilee urged.

'He was married to Eloise Grimshaw. She was the daughter of Lord Robert and Lady Margaret Grimshaw and the sister-in-law of Lady Jane.'

'Oh my god! So they were involved,' Jubilee exclaimed, a satisfying smile spread across her face. 'There's your proof Alex.'

'What did you find out about him?' Henry asked.

'His name was Patrick Mallard and at the time of the robberies he was thirty-five years old. I've downloaded a couple of pictures of him,' Meg said, producing her iPad and showing everyone a picture of Mallard.

'His death was recorded in 1940. It says he was killed in South Africa, supposedly in a diamond mine explosion. However, his body was never recovered. I did find a death certificate for him, recorded in 1947, when he was officially declared dead.'

'I doubt he was ever in South Africa,' Alex interjected. 'I've not heard back yet from my lawyer, I'll chase him up.'

'Well, if he didn't die in a mining accident, could he be the other man found in the sewer? You mentioned there's no record of him after 1939,' Henry asked. 'Was his body brought back to England?'

'I don't think so,' Meg replied.

'How can we find out?' Jubilee asked.

'There would have to be shipping records and manifests. Either from a plane or a ship,' Susan said, eager to contribute to the investigation.

'Wait, wait a minute. Show me his picture again, Meg,' Jubilee asked urgently. Meg handed over the iPad.

'Do you remember the description of the three men who were seen fighting in the Plymouth alley? It was in your grandmother's correspondence you showed us the other night, Henry. One was very tall, and broad chested with red hair.'

They all looked at the photo of Patrick Mallard standing beside his wife, Eloise on their wedding day. He stood easily over six foot, with a broad chest and shoulders. However, they couldn't confirm his hair colour from the black and white photo. Meg quickly opened up more saved pictures, which she had found on the internet and showed everyone pictures of his two sons, standing with their elderly mother. Both had red hair.

'That must be him,' Jubilee said. 'He has to be the second man in the sewer. More importantly, I think we've just uncovered the true identity of our great-grandfather. It has to be Hughie McBean, Meg. By elimination, he's the only one left.'

Meg nodded her agreement, silently proud of herself.

'What the hell was Mallard doing in Plymouth?' Henry asked, wondering what part he may have played in his great-uncle's murder nearly a century ago.

'Maybe he followed McBean down there after the robbery,' Susan suggested. 'Or, maybe, they were escaping together. What if the Grimshaws were unaware of the robberies, and it was Mallard who committed them, or at least the last one, and then fled with his share of the jewellery? Maybe Hughie double-crossed him in Plymouth.'

Alex pointed out, 'But that doesn't explain how the emerald earrings ended up in Lady Grimshaw's possession. They had to be involved, in some way. Maybe Mallard followed McBean to Plymouth to silence him.'

Meg admitted that they may never know for sure, but as she looked over at Henry and Susan, she could see the disappointment on their faces. 'We still don't know how Jack Hawthorn fits into our story. I'm sorry you guys. He may have just been an innocent bystander, or someone Hughie lured into the alley for his passport and ticket.'

Henry conceded that the truth may never been known, but he concurred that if Mallard's family concealed his disappearance by claiming he went to South Africa and died in an accident, then they must know what happened.

'How did Mallard's family know he was dead?' he asked.

'Good question,' Jubilee replied.

Susan suggested another explanation. 'Maybe they hoped he was dead. He might have been as shady as Hughie McBean and when Mallard saw an opportunity to make some money, he schemed to steal the ruby set at Harrowgate Hall. All the while, the Grimshaws saw an opportunity to commit fraud by claiming insurance on items not stolen. Unless Mallard actually stole from his own family and fled? Then, when World War Two broke out they saw an opportunity to declare him dead after seven years. I doubt the police would have investigated too enthusiastically. They would not have questioned Lord Grimshaw's word.'

'It's plausible,' Meg said. 'Still, without proof, we can't know what the Grimshaws got up to and we certainly can't accuse them of anything.'

Jubilee asked Meg if she had located any family members for Hughie McBean.

'I haven't. He could've been a loner,' Meg said, 'with no family to tie him down. I doubt he had a wife and children. I should have found them by now.'

Meg agreed to keep searching, but deep down she hoped she wouldn't uncover a relative. She didn't want to add bigamy to Hughie's sinister list of felonies.

'Maybe it's best to let sleeping dogs lie, Jubilee,' Susan suggested. 'You could stir up a hornet's nest messing into people's lives.'

Once the meeting drew to an end, everyone returned to their respective jobs. Jubilee went back to the kitchen, while

Henry needed to check that a blown fuse had been fixed in a guest bedroom. Susan headed to her office to process a pile of invoices, and Alex had to call her lawyer, Lockwood. Meg decided to go back up to her bedroom to continue her research.

Meg walked back through the foyer, heading towards the lift, but stopped when the concierge called out her name.

'There is a woman here to see you,' the concierge said as she approached the desk. 'She wouldn't give her name, but she's sitting over there.'

The concierge nodded towards the seating area near the fireplace. Meg immediately recognised Ms Upton.

Meg walked over and sat down in the chair across from Ms Upton.

'I didn't expect to see you again. A phone call would've been sufficient,' Meg said kindly.

'I wanted to hand something to you personally. I should have done something with it years ago, but I was a coward. It's about time I stood on my own two feet.' With that, Ms Upton opened her handbag and pulled out a large brown envelope. She handed it to Meg and said, 'let justice be done.'

Meg opened the envelope and found a woman's diary inside. When she opened the front cover, she read the inscription:

Diary of Lady Jane Grimshaw, 1939

She then read the note, written by Lady Jane Grimshaw.

Dear Mabel,

Please keep my diary safe, and let justice be done.

'So you had it all this time?' Meg asked.

'Yes. Lady Jane gave it to my mother the day before she committed suicide.'

'What?'

'It was not an accident. Lord Grimshaw told the police it was, but he lied. She felt trapped in that retched house, and finally one day went down to the lake and drowned herself.'

Meg looked down at Ms Upton's suitcase.

'Lady Jane couldn't escape that house, but I can, and finally have.'

Meg had assumed she was checking in. Meg had seriously underestimated Ms Upton. The woman in front of her had inherited a troubling story many years ago. It wasn't an easy thing to turn your back on your life. All Ms Upton had to show for her life was one solitary suitcase.

'Thank you.'

Ms Upton abruptly stood up to leave, making Meg stand too. She offered her a room at the hotel for the night, but Ms Upton declined the offer. The thought of Ms Upton starting her life all over again, alone, at her age made Meg feel lonely and homesick.

'What will you do now?' Meg asked, dreading the answer.

'I'll be fine. While I've spent my life serving others under that roof, I saved every penny. Now, I'm going to put it to good use. I'm going to live for myself.'

Meg smiled at her courage and said, 'If you're ever in Australia, I'd be disappointed if you didn't come and pay me a visit.'

Ms Upton returned Meg's smile. She picked up her suitcase and walked towards the foyer. Meg called after her.

'I don't even know your first name!'

'It's Georgina. But you can call me Georgie, or Ms Upton is fine.'

Meg watched after her until she was outside the hotel, thinking all the while how courageous she was. Clutching the diary tightly, Meg ran through the lobby and into the dining room, which was being set up for dinner. She quickly walked into the kitchen where she found Jubilee, busy preparing quails. A crunching sound made her cringe. She learnt long ago, from David Attenborough, that everything on this planet eats everything else. Her mother kept chickens, but only for the eggs. She would never eat chicken again if she thought her mother was capable of killing a family pet. Especially since Meg and her sisters had named them all.

Meg hesitated before she showed Jubilee the diary. She had second thoughts about telling her now. She wasn't sure what was in it and could see Jubilee was in her element, so decided not to interrupt her. She simply told Jubilee she would catch up with her after dinner and left the kitchen quickly after hearing the crushing sounds of more tiny bones.

Stepping outside into the garden, Meg found a spare table and ordered a drink, before settling in for a long read. She opened the diary and read the note once again.

Let justice be done.

As she turned the pages, Meg could see that Lady Jane's handwriting was delicate and articulate up until late April 1939, when it became more erratic and rushed, as if she had a lot on her mind. Meg wondered if she ever had anyone to confide in, in that big unfriendly house. Her only outlet was possibly her diary. Meg began reading from January and continued through until the day after the robbery.

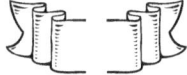

April 27, 1939

I scarcely know where to begin.

Last night, we had a break-in. The thieves were interrupted while trying to break open the safe in the drawing room. I was fortunate that my jewellery was secure in a small safe in my bedroom. I had not fallen asleep when the commotion began. Robert and Patrick armed themselves and chased after the intruders. When they returned hours later, they had captured one of them. Mallard was his usual brutish self and dragged the poor man back inside the manor. I expected them to call the police, but they did not.

When I questioned Robert about it, he told me to go back to bed and never mention it again. Right then, I knew something was wrong. I suspect Robert killed one of them. He has been overly proud of himself all day, boasting profoundly.

This afternoon, Robert, Patrick, and the thief left the manor. I hoped, rather than believed, that Robert took the thief to the police. Eloise claimed to know nothing about last night. I'm uncertain what to think. She's lying again.

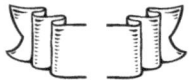

April 28, 1939

Robert hasn't returned yet. I'm not sure what to do. Secretly, I hope he never returns, but there must be an explanation for his absence. I asked Hardcastle to call the police, but he said his Lordship had everything under control. He is always the astute and loyal butler to Robert. Eloise hasn't heard from Patrick, she told me to be patient and wait for their return. I found blood in the cellar today, I believe it belongs to the thief. Eloise knows more than she's letting on. My children are safe, that's all I care about. I dread to think what happened to that man.

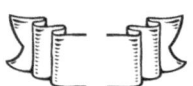

Meg continued reading, becoming more intrigued by Lady Jane's misfortunes.

April 30, 1939

Robert returned without Patrick, looking more dishevelled and panicked than I've ever seen him. He told Eloise that Patrick was dead, claiming he was killed by the thief as he escaped. Eloise has been hysterical all day. Robert has refused to speak to the police. I think he used this man to break into Harrowgate Hall two nights ago.

I can't believe what is happening. Robert instructed Eloise to say that if anyone asks about Patrick's whereabouts, she was to say he left England for South Africa, to check on his mining interests. He made it clear if she expects to be financially compensated she was to do as she was told. Of course, she agreed.

My husband must be in more debt than I otherwise thought. When will this nightmare end?

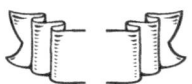

As Meg read Lady Jane's diary entries, she could feel her regrets, loneliness and sadness in every paragraph. Meg felt her anguish as the pages revealed more of her despair. It wasn't until May 5 that Meg finally had proof of the Grimshaws' fraud.

May 5, 1939

I loathe Robert. I wish it had been him and not Patrick who died.

Robert finally called the police and reported the break-in. He informed them that the thieves had stolen cash and jewellery. He had only noticed them missing today. The police told him they found a man's body along the roadside who they believe was involved. Robert gave them a list of the stolen items. I couldn't believe the condescension of the man. He wanted a police report to file an insurance claim. After the police left, I went upstairs to check my safe – it was empty. He took my grandmother's diamond necklace and earrings, along with numerous other pieces of jewellery. I can't believe he did that. I demanded them back, but he said they were already sold. I threatened to go to the police and expose him for what he was. He slapped me hard across the face.

I'm frightened of him. How do I escape this nightmare?

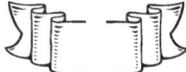

When war was declared on September 3, 1939, Lady Jane's diary entries profoundly expressed her fears and anxieties. She feared for her children, and for her country and, ultimately for her own life. On November 21, all she wrote was, *When will it all end?*

Meg read every entry up until December 31, and by then she was in tears. She couldn't imagine the mental suffering and emotional pain Lady Jane endured until her death in 1941. Meg wished she'd had the diaries pertaining to the last two years of Lady Jane's life. When Meg turned over the last page of the diary, she noticed a note written in a scribbled handwriting taped to the back page. It was dated the day of Lady Jane's death, September 9, 1941. As she read it, a chill ran down her spine. It was her suicide note.

Meg was left to wonder if the events of April 26, precipitated Lady Jane's downward spiral and mental state. But she also believed that Robert Grimshaw was a prick and solely responsible for his wife's misery. However, she wasn't too sure if Jubilee would see it that way. She didn't want her cousin to feel guilty and carry the burden of responsibility for Hughie McBean's part in Lady Jane's tragic fate. Even if it was just a small part.

*   *   *

July 15 – Saturday evening – Henry & Susan's sitting room

Meg arrived with Lady Jane's diary and Jubilee's laptop. Meanwhile, Susan was making everyone a drink as they waited for Henry's arrival. He had one last emergency to address before joining them.

When Henry entered the room, he felt a brief buzz seeing Jubilee again. Susan handed him a beer, and they all settled in to hear Meg's latest news.

'Why didn't you tell me earlier?' Jubilee asked.

'Because you were busy, and I wanted to understand the contents of the diary before sharing it with you all. I knew Georgina was hiding something,' Meg explained.

'Who's Georgina?' asked Henry, a little confused.

'Ms Upton, Henry, do keep up will you?' chided his sister.

'Please don't keep me in suspense any longer,' Jubilee pleaded.

Meg opened the diary and re-read the passages that were relevant to their research.

'It confirms what your grandfather suspected all along, Alex. The robbery was an inside job, but it was the Grimshaws and not the Henley-Smiths who were responsible. Eloise and her husband, Patrick Mallard, were at the family estate the night of the robbery. Robert and Patrick saw an opportunity to rid themselves of debt, and possibly offered Hughie a chance to gain his freedom if he helped steal the rubies from Harrowgate Hall. But I doubt they ever intended to let Hughie McBean live after that final robbery.'

'I bloody knew it,' Alex remarked.

'Yet, it seems Hughie managed to escape from them, because he fled to Australia a few days later, using my great-uncle's passport,' Henry said.

Jubilee placed her hand on Henry's, feeling a wave of sympathy for him since they still had no answers to explain Jack Hawthorn's death.

Meg continued reading aloud from July 1939.

I barely speak to Robert anymore, and yet I cannot leave. I'm afraid of what lies ahead. I now believe Robert killed Patrick. If not, Patrick must have escaped from this horrendous family. I no longer know what the truth is anymore. There's nowhere I can go to be free and safe. War is coming. I feel trapped, and I'm drowning. The Germans are knocking at our gates and I fear what the future holds. I'm afraid for my children. I feel nothing but dread.

God help me.

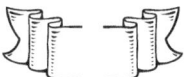

Meg finally read the note written at the back of the diary. It was the last diary entry written by Lady Jane.

Mrs Upton, please keep this journal safe. You're the only person in this house that I can trust. You've always been kind to me during my years here. You'll know what to do with it when the time comes. Please tell my children that I love them very much. I beg their forgiveness for what I must do.

God forgive me.

Everyone remained silent for a moment, each silently absorbing the depth of Lady Jane's last thoughts.

Meg recounted some passages from the diary she had read earlier, explaining to everyone that Lady Jane's diary revealed Mallard was in serious debt and that Lord Grimshaw wasn't willing to bail him out any more. He'd already spent the inheritance that his wife Eloise received upon their marriage. But Lady Jane uncovered that it was Mallard who had schemed to steal the rubies worn by Cecelia Henley-Smith on her birthday, and Lord Grimshaw went along with his scheme for a cut.

Meg continued to explain to everyone that Mallard told his brother-in-law that he had a contact who would buy the jewellery. A few weeks later, Sir Malcolm Henley-Smith arrived and accused Mallard of the theft, because he recognised the name that the servant overheard. Robert told Sir Malcolm that Mallard was dead, which led Lady Jane to believe her husband was involved somehow. Both men came to a mutual understanding, most likely involving false insurance claims and a cash settlement.

'So, both men went along with the tale that Patrick Mallard had fled to South Africa, and Sir Malcolm later signed Patrick Mallard's death certificate without question. *Nice*,' Jubilee remarked.

'It certainly appears that way,' Meg replied.

'Is this diary enough proof, Alex?' Susan asked.

'It might be construed as hearsay, but it might carry some weight,' she replied.

'Either way, Lady Jane was aware of her husband's actions, and despised him for it,' Jubilee said, shaking her head.

At that moment, Meg's mobile chimed. It was a message from her mother, urging her to call back 'ASAP'. Meg quickly opened the laptop. When her mother appeared on the video call, Meg introduced her to Henry, Susan and Alex.

'I have heard from the Unclaimed Property Office. They finally released the contents of Jack Jones's safety deposit box. They were proud to say that it was one of their oldest.'

'Was it the remaining jewellery?' piped up Jubilee, excitedly.

'No, sorry love. It contained a letter that Jack wrote to Mary, which he must have felt needed to be hidden away in the safety deposit box.'

'Why didn't they just contact her and give her the letter when the fees stopped being paid?' Meg asked, shaking her head in astonishment.

'They claimed they sent out many letters to Mary Jones after Jack died, but she ignored all their requests. After reading his letter, I'd say she wanted nothing to do with Jack Jones's past.'

'So you've read the letter?' Jubilee asked.

'Oh yes! You're not going to believe what it says.'

'Please Mum, don't keep us in suspense,' implored Meg.

'It's a confession.'

'A what?' Meg asked, surprised.

'Oh my god!' Jubilee said, bewildered.

'Plus, he admits to stealing a lot more jewellery than what was discovered in your garden, Jubilee. He buried it before he fled from Plymouth. He's provided details of its location. You'll need to go there and find it.'

'Holy shit!' exclaimed Meg, laughing.

'Please read the note, Aunt Joan.'

Everyone sat anxiously, squashed together on the sofa, their eyes glued to the monitor, as they eagerly waited for Joan to read a confession written over 80 years ago.

Joan began.

My name is not Jack Jones, but Hughie McBean.

I was a thief, and a bloody goodn at that. But the devil caught up with me and Tommy Fields. We robbed a few estates down the west coast of England in 39 but got caught at Grimshaw Manor in Bath. We legged it but they chased us and Tommy got himself shot by his bloody Lordship in the woods. The bastard just let him bleed to death. Took him an hour to die. They took what we had on us. Not much about £20 which I nicked from the last house we robbed and Tommy had a couple of small pieces, rings and earrings stuffed in his pockets.

I expected them to call the old bill but they never did. Instead, I was taken back to their home and locked up below ground until Lord Grimshaw and Patrick Mallard made me an offer I couldn't refuse. They wanted me to rob an estate in Somerset. They said if I did, they'd let me go, and I could keep whatever was in the safe except the ruby set. They said they would tell the coppers only Tommy robbed them.

I may be a thief but I ain't no fool. I knew they would kill me either way, so I said yes. But Mallard insisted on entering the house with me so I couldn't leg it. His bloody Lordship drove us in his car to the edge of the estate. I went along with them, but I had to think quick so when the job was done, I made a ruckus which woke the house. We ran through the kitchen and I saw a kitchen maid so I yelled out Mallard's name, call it insurance. He weren't happy I did it, but if they killed me at least they'd have his name. I grabbed a knife when I ran through the kitchen and turned it on him once we was clear. I tied him up and legged it.

Now me and Tommy always robbed two or three houses at a time. We buried the stolen goods from the previous job before committing the next one in case we get nicked. We fenced them, then when the money ran out, we started again. So I headed back and dug up the stuff we stole from the previous three robberies. Then I headed down to Plymouth as it was time to leave England. I needed cash and a new passport so I called my bagman, Claude Blackman. He always paid well. I told him where I was and he said he'd come to Plymouth and bring me my money, but he didn't turn up. Next night I left a pub but was set on by Patrick Mallard. They found me. That bastard Blackman must have told him where I was. Don't know how he knew Mallard.

Anyway, we fought, he was getting the better of me. I saw his Lordship at the end of the alley watching. They wanted them rubies. Mallard was about to stab me when a young man jumped him and pulled him off me. Mallard stabbed him instead. Mallard was shocked by what he did and that was my chance to take the knife from him and stick it to him. His Lordship ran off. Both men lay dead in the alley. I wasn't gonna be hanged for a murder I didn't commit. Although Mallard was self-defence. So I dragged both men to the manhole cover and dropped them in the sewer. I didn't like putting them in there but I had no choice. I thought they would be found once I left Plymouth. I frisked Mallard and the young man before putting them in the sewer. Mallard had nothing but £10 on him but the young man, Jack Hawthorn was his name, had a passport and ticket for a ship leaving for Australia in two days.

This was my only chance so I took it. I had my photo taken and changed it for the one in Jack's passport and altered the birthdate. I went to Wembury and buried most of the jewellery near the old church by the beach. There was a new grave recently occupied in the churchyard so I buried most of the jewellery in the upturned soil. I couldn't take all the jewellery with me in case I got searched but I sewed some into my clothes.

If I don't ever get back there to retrieve the rest, that's where you'll find it.

Look for the grave of Finnegan Duffy. Says, 1893 – 1939, He died as he lived, a drunkard.

He's looking after it for me.

I'm sorry about Jack Hawthorn. He was a good bloke for helping me. But they would have hanged me if I stayed. My word against a Lord, no chance. I read later in a paper about Tommy's death. It implied I did it and fled with his share of the loot. And they think I'm scum.

It's been twenty years now and I've got a new life here in Australia. I haven't thieved since arriving here. I've got a wife and two children. I sold a few more pieces of jewellery over the years when times was tough. The rest I've buried in the garden. Ten paces north of the shed. Two paces from the fence.

*Let it be known, my wife and children
had no part in this.*

This is a true account for what it's worth.

Hughie McBean

Jubilee covered her mouth in disbelief. She had finally uncovered the truth. She turned to Harry and said, 'I'm so sorry about Jack, but at least you understand how and why he died. He was a brave young man.'

Everyone remained silent for the longest time. Nobody knew what to say.

'Earth to Jubilee,' said Joan. 'This is the evidence you've been waiting for. Get yourselves down to Wembury and find the rest of that jewellery. I checked, and the church is still there.'

Meg, Jubilee, Susan, Henry, and Alex exchanged glances before bursting into laugher.

'Oh, god. We can't just go digging up a grave. We'd get arrested,' Susan protested.

'No, but you can alert the police, and they can do the digging,' Joan said. 'Let them determine what pieces belong to which estate.'

Jubilee fell silent. A thought was niggling at her. She pulled out her notebook and flipped through its pages until she found what she was looking for.

'I thought so!' she exclaimed. 'Meg, do you remember the jeweller we emailed that said they couldn't help us? Their name was Blackman and Chambers.'

'You're right. I thought Blackman rang a bell,' Alex said. 'Blackman and Chambers haven't been jewellers for over thirty years, but they're a diamond brokerage firm now, called Blackman and Sons. That firm had a reputation in the old days. I remember my father warning Rose and me to steer clear of them. But, as far as I know, they're kosher. If it turns out they were involved in handling stolen jewellery, the police would be keen to investigate further. They're always on the lookout for diamond smuggling, which is often tied to money laundering. I can only assume that Mallard or Lord Grimshaw knew Claude Blackman back in the day, perhaps they were school friends. Please leave Blackman to me. I'll call Lockwood and find out what measures can be taken.'

'He's all yours,' Jubilee said.

Susan asked if it could have been someone associated with Blackman that broke into their campervan and home in Bowral, looking for the jewels or, possibly clues on where to locate the rest.

'It's possible,' Meg replied, 'however, it could be anyone who knew about the robberies.'

'True,' Jubilee said, mulling over her own ideas. 'But if Claude Blackman knew Hughie McBean, his firm might know if Hughie or Tom Fields had any relatives here in England.'

'Do you really want to go down that path, Jubes?' Meg asked, shaking her head in caution. 'Maybe we should leave that alone for now.'

Jubilee conceded. She could see Meg didn't want to dig deeper into their lives. She had uncovered what she came to England to find. She finally understood the ramifications of involving another family in her great-grandfather's escapades. Meg was right. She didn't want to unearth anything else. She decided it was time to put the past to bed.

'Well you have your proof now, Alex,' Susan stated. 'Your grandfather's reputation is undeniably restored. Jack

Jones's letter, I mean Hughie's letter, proves it. The rubies will undoubtedly be returned to your family's business.'

Alex needed a moment to reply. She was overcome with joy. She had been waiting for this validation for many years. She only wished that her grandfather was alive to hear it. 'Thank you,' was all she could say as she wiped away a tear from her face.

'What will happen to the Grimshaws and Henley-Smiths? Will those families be held accountable and made liable to pay back the insurance claims for the jewellery that wasn't stolen?' Susan asked.

'I'm not sure,' Alex replied. 'Lord Giles Grimshaw and Rupert Henley-Smith haven't actually done anything wrong. Their families may have colluded to commit fraud but I think only their reputations would be put on trial. I guess it will be up to the police to investigate. It was still a lot of money back in 1939.'

Joan emailed Jack's letter to Meg. Within two days, all five amateur sleuths found themselves standing beside Finnegan Duffy's grave in the graveyard of St Werbugh's church in Wembury, Plymouth.

They eagerly waited for the police forensic team to excavate the grave. They planned to stay by Finnegan Duffy's graveside until the police found the evidence.

Meg filmed the site for her mother, who would have loved to be there.

Chapter Twenty Five

Hawthorn Hotel, Cornwall

July 19 – Wednesday, mid-morning – Day 15

Meg hugged Jubilee tightly as she said, 'I'm glad you're staying.' Meg's tears could no longer be restrained.

'It feels right, you know?' Jubilee replied, allowing her tears to run free as well.

Meg completely understood. 'It's a shame I won't be here when you return the jewellery, especially to Maryann Bishop and William Hardwick. I would have liked to have seen that.'

'I wish you could stay longer too.' Jubilee was going to miss her cousin dearly.

'Overall, only five pieces were missing from the police reports. Not including the jewellery allegedly stolen from Grimshaw Manor and Harrowgate Hall. You should be proud of yourself.'

Jubilee smiled through her tears, 'I am. We've really made a difference here, you know. I'm going to miss you so much.'

'Just remember, you can call me for a chat, anytime.'

'I know, but it's not like the real thing.'

'True, but you love it here. As soon as we landed, I could see something had changed in you, especially after meeting Henry, in person.'

'Shush,' Jubilee blushed, and quickly looked at Henry and Susan, who were standing a respectable distance from them.

Meg didn't need Jubilee to confess anything to know she was in love. Not just with Henry but England too. Meg was pleased that Jubilee had found her place in the world. She was leaving her in safe hands.

'You deserve to be happy. So, be happy!' Meg insisted and gave her cousin another warm, tight hug.

'I think I will,' she whispered back.

Henry and Susan walked over to Meg and kissed her farewell before she got into the taxi. She was going to miss all of them. They continued to wave goodbye until the car had disappeared from view.

'I'm glad you agreed to stay,' Henry told Jubilee. 'You're just what this place needs.'

'Hear, hear!' Susan agreed.

Susan walked back towards the hotel. She paused to look out across the beautiful tiered gardens and wondered where the best spot for her brother's wedding should be. She quite liked Meg's suggestion. It had been ages since she'd seen her brother this giddy over a woman. Susan decided to instigate a little matchmaking in the hope of speeding them along, otherwise, it could take years.

Henry was about to follow his sister inside, since he had yet another issue to deal with, but he hesitated and turned back to Jubilee, who was still daydreaming, long after the taxi had disappeared. Henry wrapped his arms around Jubilee to comfort her. He held her tenderly until she turned to face him and longingly kissed him gently on the lips.

Jubilee had taken the lead. It felt right. She had anticipated the dreadful feelings of loneliness and abandonment once Meg's taxi had disappeared from sight, yet they didn't come. Instead, she felt completely at ease. No anxious butterflies, just serene calmness. She had solved the mystery of her great-grandfather, and in doing so, given herself a new found freedom, without feeling one step behind everyone else. She kissed Henry again.

As she re-entered the hotel, Jubilee began twirling her grandmother's ring on her finger. She stopped to look down at it. A strange familiarity that she couldn't quite put her finger on, washed over her.

Then the penny dropped, Jubilee laughed to herself and kissed her ring. She stepped inside the hotel, grateful that her captive spirit was finally free from its cage.

Chapter Twenty Six

Grimshaw Manor, Bath

July 18 – Tuesday afternoon – Day 14

Louis yelled into his phone, 'Why the hell did you let your bloody wife wear those emerald earrings?'

'I didn't know they were stolen,' retorted Giles sharply. 'I thought they belonged to my mother.'

'They have proof. My lawyer said it's documented in a diary. Your grandmother's diary! What do you know about that?'

'Shit! It must be her diary from 1939,' Giles said. 'It's been missing for years. I thought my grandfather had destroyed it, along with the last two years of her life.'

'Well! Who's had it all those years?'

Giles remained silent, contemplating who his grandmother had trusted enough to keep it safe.

'I'll find out. But don't call me again. We're finished.'

Giles Grimshaw decided to distance himself from his old school friend, Louis Blackman. He accepted severing ties was necessary to salvage his family's reputation. Giles looked at his wife, and demanded to know why she felt the need to wear *those* bloody earrings and be photographed in the act, no less? He wasn't about to lay any blame at his own feet.

'What's the point of having expensive jewellery if I can't show them off, darling?' Joanna replied. 'No one had ever noticed or questioned them until now, not even you. Regretfully, I'm going to miss them. They always managed to bring out the green in my eyes.'

Giles cursed under his breath. 'If my grandmother gave her journal to someone, I think I know who it was.'

Joanna recognised her husband's growing anger. She decided to let setting dogs lie and speak no more of the events in 1939. Gossip would pass as it always did. She wondered which friend she could throw under the bus, to deflect attention from her husband's family indiscretions for the time being.

'Where is Ms Upton?' Giles rang the bell, but only the housemaid came to attend him.

'I'm sorry sir, she left on Saturday morning. I believe she left you a letter, it's on the table in the front lobby.'

'Well, get it for me, you stupid girl.'

She darted out of the room to retrieve Ms Upton's letter. Once she handed it to Lord Grimshaw, she left quickly, eager to escape before he finished reading her letter.

July 15

I hereby tender my resignation.

By the time you read this letter, I will be gone from your miserable household.

Before she died, Lady Jane Grimshaw entrusted my mother with her 1939 diary, and asked her to keep it safe. When the time came, she wanted my mother to surrender it to the police. Regrettably, my mother did not. She carried the weight of that shame her entire life for not exposing Lord Grimshaw for the cad he was.

On her deathbed, I was given the diary. Sadly, I didn't know what to do with it either. It was so long ago. However, one thing you should know, your grandmother's death wasn't an accident. She committed suicide because she loathed the man she married. I guess my mother thought it better to let everyone believe she drowned by accident rather than expose Lady Jane's depression and misery to her friends, family, and especially her children.

After the visit by Jubilee Jones and Meg Forrester, I felt compelled to hand the diary over to them. They can do what my mother and I couldn't. Expose the truth about your family.

I'm off to live my own life now.

Georgina Upton

Giles Grimshaw screwed up the letter and threw it across the room. He knocked his glass of whiskey off the table beside him as he stormed out of the room. After he departed, Lady Joanna picked up the letter and read it quietly to herself. She was well aware of the family she had married into and was determined not to share Lady Jane's fate.

Chapter Twenty Seven

The Ink in the Quill, Bowral

July 22 – Saturday morning

*M*eg was glad to be back home, surrounded by the familiar comfort of her beloved books. She eagerly anticipated the arrival of her newly acquired books during her visits to many of England's antique bookshops.

As she strolled around her bookshop, she checked the shelves to make sure everything was in order. She had bought gifts for everyone, especially for her mum and Jodie for taking care of her bookshop. As she sat down at the counter, going through the mail that had been waiting for her, she became a little maudlin herself. She missed Jubilee and felt unexpectedly alone.

Meg thought about her flight home. She had spent many hours making extensive notes of their adventure around England. When she finally rested her head back in the chair, she couldn't sleep. She felt restless and thought about what she should do next. Books had always been her passion, but now she wanted more.

Her thoughts were interrupted as the front door opened, and Billy walked in carrying two coffees and two pastries from her favourite patisserie. Meg was flattered by his awkwardness, as he tried to close the door without spilling the coffee.

He smiled back at her and said, 'I thought you could use a coffee, in case you were still suffering jetlag?'

'Perfect timing!' Meg said. 'I had a call from Alex Everett last night. Her lawyer found a connection between Mallard, Lord Grimshaw, and Blackman. They all co-owned that ill-fated diamond mine in South Africa. The same one where Lord Grimshaw claimed Mallard was killed.'

'Everything is falling into place. Scotland Yard told us they served a search warrant at Blackman and Sons, no doubt instigated by Starr and Everett. I can't say much more, but I think they've found more than they bargained for.'

'My god … so it's really happening then.'

'I'm afraid so. The police also visited Grimshaw Manor and handed them a subpoena for the emerald earrings Lady Grimshaw was wearing in those photos you provided. Of course, they can't be charged with anything, since the fraud was perpetrated by the late Lord Robert Grimshaw, but they can certainly seize the emerald earrings and return them to their rightful owners.'

Meg laughed. 'I bet they weren't too happy about that.'

'I wouldn't think they were. Although, they co-operated to prevent any more scandal.'

'What about the Henley-Smiths?'

'The police only have Lady Jane's diary to insinuate they were involved in fraud. They can't prove anything beyond reasonable doubt so they won't be investigated. The police only have the rubies from that estate as the rest of their alleged stolen jewellery is missing.'

Meg thanked Billy for all his help, especially the background searches she had asked for. They chatted for another half hour, between Meg serving the customers who entered the shop.

When Billy finally said goodbye, he seemed nervous as he approached the shop door. He paused as he held the door handle, then turned back to Meg. He asked her if she would like to have dinner with him next Saturday.

Meg was flattered by his nervousness. She let him stew for a long two seconds before she answered yes.

'Just don't bring any paintbrushes with you, Willy,' she said, smiling.

Later that evening at home, Meg sat at her desk above her bookshop and opened her new computer. She placed her notebook next to her, along with a glass of wine and a box of chocolates. Then, taking a deep breath, she started typing.

THE JEWEL THIEF

By
Meg Forrester

CHAPTER ONE

Plymouth, April 1939

He ran faster than his heart would allow. His heavy rucksack weighed him down, he was sweating profusely. He darted through the woods using the trees for cover. The night air had the stench of death in it, but it wouldn't be his. He had to get to the coast, from there he would find a ship and get off this accursed island...

The End